Christ
Legends

Selma Lagerlöf

Translated by Velma Swanston Howard and Polly Lawson
Illustrated by Ronald Heuninck

First published in Swedish as *Kristuslegender* 1904
"The Christmas Rose" was first published in *En Saga om en Sage* 1908
First published in English as *Christ Legends* by T Werner Laurie, London 1937

Previously published by Floris Books as *The Emperor's Vision*

This edition published by Floris Books, Edinburgh 2013
© Floris Books, Edinburgh 2002, 2013

British Library CIP Data available
ISBN 978-086315-981-7
Printed in Great Britain
bt TJ International Ltd, Cornwall

Contents

The Holy Night

When I was five years old I was very sad. I may not have felt so sad since.

My grandmother died. Until then, she used to sit every day on the corner sofa in her room and tell stories.

Grandmother told story after story from morning till night, and we sat beside her, quite still, and listened. It was wonderful! No other children had such happy times as we did.

I don't remember much about my grandmother. But I do remember that she had very beautiful snow-white hair, and that she stooped when she walked, and that she sat all day long knitting socks.

And I even remember that when she had finished a story, she used to lay her hand on my head and say, "All this is true, as true as that I see you and you see me."

I also remember that she could sing songs, but she didn't sing them every day. One of the songs was about a knight and a sea-troll, and the chorus went like this: "It blows cold, cold weather at sea."

I remember a little prayer she taught me, and the verse of a hymn.

I have just a dim and hazy memory of the stories she told me, and there's only one that I remember well enough to tell. It's a little story about Jesus' birth.

Well, that's nearly all I remember about my grandmother, except for one thing: the great loneliness I felt when she was gone.

I remember the morning when the corner sofa stood empty and after that were days that never seemed to come to an end. That I remember. That I shall never forget.

And I remember being afraid to kiss Grandmother's hand after she'd died, until we children were told that it would be our last chance to thank her for all the pleasure she'd given us.

And I remember how Grandmother and her stories and songs were driven from the homestead, shut up in a long black casket, and how they never came back again.

Something was gone from our lives. The door to a beautiful, enchanted world – where before we could come and go freely – had been closed. Now no one knew how to open that door.

Little by little, we learned to play with dolls and toys, and to live like other children. And it seemed as though we no longer missed our grandmother, or remembered her.

But even today – after forty years – as I gather together legends about Christ that I heard in the East, the little legend of Jesus' birth that my grandmother used to tell comes to me, and I feel impelled to tell it once again.

It was Christmas Day and everyone had driven to church except Grandmother and me. We were all alone in the house. We weren't allowed to go along because one of us was too old and the other was too young. And we were both sad because we wouldn't hear the singing or see the Christmas candles.

But as we sat there, feeling lonely, Grandmother began to tell a story...

"There was a man," she said, "who went out on a dark night to borrow live coals to kindle a fire. He went from hut to hut and knocked. 'Dear friends, help me!' he said. 'My wife has just given birth to a child, and I must make a fire to warm her and the little one.'

"But it was late and everyone was asleep. No one replied.

"The man walked and walked. At last he saw the gleam of a fire a long way off. He headed towards the glimmer until he came to a fire burning out in the open. Sheep slept around the fire, while an old shepherd sat and watched over the flock.

"Three big dogs lay asleep at the shepherd's feet. All three woke when the man approached and opened their great jaws to bark, but no sound came out. The man saw the hair on their backs bristle and their sharp, white teeth glisten in the firelight. They dashed towards him. One bit his leg, another bit his hand and the third clung to his throat. But their jaws wouldn't close and their teeth wouldn't cut, and the man came to no harm.

"Now the man needed to get to the fire to collect the coals, but the sheep lay back to back, blocking his way. He stepped on their backs and walked over them and up to the fire. Not one of the animals awoke or moved."

At this point I couldn't help breaking in. "Why didn't they wake up, Grandmother?" I asked.

"That you shall hear in a moment," she said, and went on with her story.

"When the man had almost reached the fire, the shepherd looked up. He was a surly, unfriendly old man. And when he saw the strange man coming, he seized the long, spiked staff that he used to tend his flock, and threw it at him. The staff flew towards the man, then swerved to one side and whizzed past him, far out into the meadow."

"Grandmother," I interrupted again, "why didn't the staff hit the man?"

Grandmother did not bother to answer, but continued her story.

"Now the man came up to the shepherd and said to him, 'Good man, help me – lend me some hot coals. My wife has just given birth to a child, and I must make a fire to warm her and the little one.'

"The shepherd wanted to say no, but then he thought about what he'd seen: the dogs couldn't hurt the man; the sheep hadn't woken when he walked on them, and the staff wouldn't strike him. The shepherd was a little bit frightened, and he dared not deny the man what he asked for.

"'Take as much as you need!' he said.

"The fire was nearly burned out. There were no logs or branches left, only a big heap of live coals, and the stranger had neither spade nor shovel to carry them with.

"When the shepherd saw this, he said again, 'Take as much as you need!' He was glad that the man wouldn't be able to.

"But the man bent down, picked coals from the ashes with his bare hands, and laid them in his robe. He didn't burn his hands when he touched them, nor did the coals scorch his robe. He carried them away as if they had been nuts or apples."

"Grandma," I interrupted for the third time, "why didn't the coals burn the man?"

"That you shall hear," said Grandmother, and went on.

"And when the shepherd, who was such a cruel and hard-hearted man, saw all this, he began to wonder to himself, 'What kind of a night is this, when dogs don't bite, sheep aren't scared, the staff doesn't kill, nor hot coals burn?' He called the stranger back, and asked, 'What kind of a night is this? Why does everything show you compassion?'

"The man said, 'I can't tell you if you yourself don't see it.' And he hurried away to get back to his wife and child.

"But the shepherd was determined to find out what all this meant, so he followed the man to where he was staying.

"When they arrived, the shepherd saw the man's wife and baby lying in a mountain cave, with nothing except cold, bare stone walls. He was worried that the poor child might freeze to death in the icy cave and, although he was a hard man, he was touched and decided to help. He loosened the knapsack from his shoulder, and took out a soft, white sheepskin. He gave it to the man for the child to sleep on.

"As soon as he showed that he, too, could be kind, his eyes were opened. He saw what he couldn't see before, and heard what he couldn't hear before.

"All around him stood a ring of small, silver-winged angels holding harps, singing boldly that tonight the saviour was born who would save the world from its sins.

"Then he understood that the dogs, sheep, staff and all other things were so happy tonight that they didn't want to cause any harm.

"And the angels were not only around the shepherd – he saw them everywhere. They sat inside the cave, they stood outside on the mountain, and they flew under the heavens. They came marching in great processions, and as they passed, they paused to glance at the child.

"There was such merriment and so many joyful songs to play! The shepherd was so happy because his eyes had been opened, that he fell upon his knees and thanked God."

Here Grandmother sighed and said, "We might also see what

9

the shepherd saw, because the angels fly down from heaven every Christmas Eve, if only we could see them."

Then Grandmother laid her hand on my head, and said, "You must remember, all this is true, as true as that I see you and you see me. The truth is not revealed by the light of lamps or candles, and it doesn't depend upon the sun and moon; we need eyes like the shepherd's that can see God's glory."

The Emperor's Vision

When Augustus was emperor in Rome and Herod was king in Jerusalem, a very great and holy night sank down over the earth. It was the darkest night anyone had ever seen, as if the whole earth had fallen into a deep cellar. It was impossible to distinguish water from land or find your way on a familiar road, because not a single ray of light came from heaven. All the stars stayed at home in their own houses, and the fair moon hid her face.

The silence and stillness were as deep as the darkness. The rivers didn't flow, the wind didn't stir, and even the aspen leaves had stopped quivering. Anyone who walked beside the sea would have found that the waves no longer crashed upon the shore; anyone who wandered in the desert would have noticed that the sand no longer crunched under his feet. Everything was as still as stone, so as not to disturb the holy night.

The grass was afraid to grow, the dew couldn't fall, and the flowers dared not share their perfume. The wild beasts didn't hunt, the snakes didn't sting, and the dogs didn't bark. Even inanimate things refused to be involved in evil deeds on this holy night: no false key could have picked a lock, and no knife could have drawn a drop of blood.

In Rome, on this very night, a small group of people came from the emperor's palace at the Palatine and took the path across the Forum that led to Capitoline Hill. The senators had suggested building a temple to Emperor Augustus on Rome's sacred hill, but Augustus had not immediately given his consent. Would the gods be happy for him to have a temple next to theirs? He planned to ask them through offering a sacrifice. It was the emperor who, accompanied by a few trusted friends, was on his way that evening to perform this sacrifice.

Augustus let his friends carry him in a litter because he was old and it was an effort to climb the long stairs leading to the Capitol. He himself held the cage with the doves for the sacrifice. No priests or soldiers or senators accompanied him, only his nearest friends. Torch-bearers led the way through the night's darkness and slaves followed behind, carrying the tripod, knives, charcoal, sacred fire and all the other things needed for the sacrifice.

The emperor and his faithful followers chatted happily, so none of them noticed the infinite silence and stillness of the night. Only when they'd reached the highest point of Capitoline Hill, and the spot where they planned to build the temple, did it dawn on them that something unusual was happening.

Up on the very edge of the cliff they saw the most remarkable figure. At first they thought it was an old, distorted olive trunk; then perhaps an ancient stone figure from the temple of Jupiter that had wandered out onto the cliff. Finally they realised it could only be an old sibyl.

They had never seen anything so aged, weather-beaten and giant. This old prophet was awe-inspiring! If the emperor had not been present, they would all have fled to their homes.

"It is she," they whispered to each other, "who has lived as many years as there are grains of sand on her native shores. Why has she come out of her cave tonight? What does she – who writes her prophecies on leaves for the wind to carry to the intended person – foretell for the emperor and the empire?"

They were so terrified that if the sibyl had stirred they would have dropped on their knees with their foreheads pressed against the earth. But she sat still, as though lifeless. Crouching upon the outermost edge of the cliff, and shading her eyes with her hand, she peered out into the night as if she were searching for something far away. She could see things on a night like this!

At that moment the emperor and his followers realised how profound the darkness was. They couldn't see even a hand's width in front of then. And what stillness! What silence! They couldn't even hear the river Tiber's hollow murmur. The air seemed to suffocate them, cold sweat broke out on their foreheads, and their hands were weak and numb. They feared that some dreadful disaster was looming.

But they didn't show their fear, and they all told the emperor that this was a good omen. All nature held its breath to greet a new god.

They advised Augustus to hurry with the sacrifice, and said that the old sibyl must have come out of her cave to welcome him.

But the truth was that the old sibyl was so absorbed in a vision that she didn't even know Augustus was there. She had been transported in spirit to a faraway land, where she imagined she was wandering over a great plain. She kept stubbing her foot against something in the darkness – probably grass tufts. She stooped down and felt with her hand. No, it wasn't grass, but sheep. She was walking between great sleeping flocks of sheep.

Then she noticed the shepherds' fire. It burned in the middle of the field, and she groped her way towards it. The shepherds lay asleep by the fire; the long, spiked staffs they used to defend their flocks from wild beasts lay beside them. But the little animals with glittering eyes and bushy tails that crept up to the fire, weren't they jackals? Yet the shepherds didn't throw their staffs, the dogs continued to sleep, the sheep didn't run away, and the wild animals lay down to rest beside the people.

This the sibyl saw, but she didn't see what was happening on the hill around her, as the emperor's followers raised an altar, lit charcoal and strewed incense, and the emperor took one of the doves from the cage as a sacrifice. But his hands felt so numb that he couldn't hold the bird. With one stroke of its wing, it flew off and disappeared into the night's darkness.

The courtiers glanced suspiciously at the old sibyl. Had she made the dove fly away?

They didn't know that the sibyl believed she was standing

beside the shepherds' fire, listening to a faint sound which came trembling through the dead-still night. She heard it long before she realised that it didn't come from the earth, but from the sky. At last she raised her head and saw light, shimmering figures gliding forward in the darkness. They were flocks of angels who, singing merrily, flew back and forth above the wide plain, searching for something.

While the sibyl listened to the angels' song, the emperor made preparations for a new sacrifice. He washed his hands, cleaned the altar, and picked up the other dove. But, although he held on as tightly as he could, the dove's slippery body slid from his hand, and the bird swung up into the ink-black night.

The emperor was horrified! He fell upon his knees and prayed to his protectors, asking them for strength to prevent the disaster which this night seemed to foretell.

The sibyl heard none of this. She was listening with her whole soul to the angels' song, which grew louder and louder. At last it became so powerful that it woke the shepherds. They raised themselves on their elbows and saw shining hosts of silver-white angels move through the darkness in long, swaying lines, like migrating birds. Some held lutes and cymbals in their hands; others held zithers and harps. And their song rang out as brightly as children's laughter and as carefree as the lark's trill. When the shepherds heard this, they stood up and headed to the mountain city where they lived, to tell of this miracle.

They groped their way forward on a narrow, winding path, and the sibyl followed. Suddenly it grew light on the mountain: a big, clear star shone above it, and the city on the mountain summit glittered like silver in the starlight. All the fluttering flocks of angels rushed towards the city, shouting for joy, and the shepherds hurried so quickly they almost ran. When they reached the city, they found the angels gathered by the city gate over a small, tumbledown stable with a straw roof, nestled against the bare hillside. Over it hung the star, as more and more angels came flocking. Some sat on the straw roof or the steep hillside behind the house; others hovered above the stable

on outspread wings. High, high up, the air was illuminated by sparkling wings.

The moment the star started to shine over the mountain city, all of nature woke up, and the men on Capitoline Hill couldn't help seeing it. They felt soft, delicate wings brushing against them; delicious perfumes streaming around them; trees swaying; the Tiber beginning to murmur; the stars twinkling; and suddenly the moon stood out in the sky and lit up the world. And out of the clouds the two doves came circling down and perched upon the emperor's shoulders.

When this miracle happened, Augustus rose, proud and happy, but his friends and slaves fell to their knees.

"Hail, Caesar!" they cried. "Your protector has answered you. You are the god who shall be worshipped on Capitoline Hill!"

And this cry of homage that the men gave to the emperor was so loud that the old sibyl heard it and awoke from her visions. She rose from her perch on the edge of the cliff, and came down to the people. It was as if a dark cloud had arisen from the abyss and rushed down the mountain. She was terrifying! Coarse hair hung in matted tangles around her head, her joints were swollen, and dark skin as hard as tree bark covered her body with furrow upon furrow.

Powerful and awe-inspiring, she advanced towards the emperor. With one hand she clutched his wrist, with the other she pointed towards the East.

"Look!" she commanded, and the emperor raised his eyes and saw. The heavens opened before his eyes, and he looked towards the East. He saw a lowly stable behind a steep rock wall and in the open doorway a few shepherds kneeling. Inside the stable he saw a young mother on her knees before a little child, who lay upon a bundle of straw on the floor.

And the sibyl's big, knotty fingers pointed towards the poor baby. "Hail, Caesar?" cried the sibyl, in a burst of scornful laughter. "*There* is the god who shall be worshipped on Capitoline Hill!"

Augustus shrank back from her as if she were a madwoman. But the mighty spirit of prophecy fell upon the sibyl. Her dim eyes began to burn, her hands were stretched towards heaven, her voice rang out with such resonance and power that it could have been heard over the whole world. And she spoke words which she appeared to be reading among the stars.

"Upon Capitoline Hill shall Christ – the redeemer of the world – be worshipped, but not frail mortals."

When she had said this, she strode past the terror-stricken men, walked slowly down the mountain, and disappeared.

On the following day, Augustus strictly forbade the people to raise any temple to him on Capitoline Hill. In place of it he built a sanctuary to the newborn God, and called it *Ara Coeli* – Heaven's Altar.

The Wise Men's Well

In old Judea, Drought crept, gaunt and hollow-eyed, between shrunken thistles and yellowed grass.

It was summertime. The sun beat down upon the backs of unshaded hills, and the slightest breath of wind tore up thick clouds of lime dust from the greyish-white ground. Herds stood huddled together in the valleys by dried-up streams.

Drought walked about and viewed the water supplies. He wandered over to Solomon's Pool, and sighed as he saw a small amount of water from the mountain springs. Then he journeyed down to the famous David's Well near Bethlehem, and found water even there. Finally, he shuffled towards the great highway that leads from Bethlehem to Jerusalem.

When he was about halfway there, he saw the Wise Men's Well close by the roadside. He noticed at a glance that it was almost dry. He sat down on the well's rim, made from a single hollowed-out stone, and looked into the well. The shining mirrored surface, which was usually near the opening, had sunk deep down, and the dirt and slime at the bottom of the well made it muddy and dirty.

When the well beheld Drought's bronzed face reflected in her clouded mirror, she shook with anguish.

"I wonder when you will be exhausted," said Drought. "Surely you don't expect to find any fresh water down there to give you new life; and as for rain – God be praised! – there can be no question of that for the next two or three months."

"You may rest happily," sighed the well, "because nothing can help me now. It would take no less than a well-spring from paradise to save me!"

"Then I will not forsake you until every drop has been drained," said Drought. He saw that the old Well was nearing its end, and he wanted to have the pleasure of seeing it die out drop by drop.

He sat down comfortably on the rim, and laughed as he heard the well sighing down there in the ground. He watched in delight as thirsty travellers came up to the well, let down the bucket, and drew it up with only a few drops of muddy water.

And so the whole day passed, and when darkness descended, Drought looked again into the well. A little water still shimmered down there. "I'll stay here all night," he cried, "so don't hurry yourself! When it's so light that I can look into you once more, I'm certain you'll be finished."

Drought curled himself up on the edge of the well, while the hot night, which was even more cruel and tormenting than the day had been, descended over Judea. Dogs and jackals howled incessantly, and thirsty cows and asses answered them from their stuffy stalls.

When the breeze stirred a little now and then, it brought no relief, but was as hot and suffocating as a great sleeping monster's panting breath. The stars shone brilliantly, and a little silvery new moon cast a pretty blue-green light over the grey hills. And in this light Drought saw a great stream of people come marching towards the Wise Men's Well.

Drought sat and gazed at the long procession, and rejoiced again at the thought of all the thirsty creatures coming to the well, who wouldn't find one drop of water. There were so many animals and drivers they could easily have emptied the well, even if it had been full. Suddenly he began to think there was something unusual, something ghost-like, about this procession, which came marching forward in the night. First all the camels appeared on a hill that loomed up, high and distinct, against the horizon; it was as though they had stepped straight down from heaven. They appeared to be larger than ordinary camels, and bore all too lightly the enormous burdens they carried.

But they seemed absolutely real – to him they were as plain as plain could be. He could even see that the three leaders were dromedaries, with grey, shiny skins; and that they were richly bridled and saddled with fringed coverings, and were ridden by handsome, noble-looking knights.

The whole procession stopped at the well. With three sharp jerks, the dromedaries lay down on the ground, and their riders dismounted.

The pack camels remained standing, and as they assembled they seemed to form a long line of necks and humps and peculiarly piled-up packs.

The riders came straight up to Drought and greeted him by laying their hands on their foreheads and chests. They wore dazzling white robes and huge turbans, on which there was a clear, glittering star that shone as if it had been taken directly from the sky.

"We come from a far-off land," said one of the strangers, "and we'd like to know if this is the Wise Men's Well?"

"It's called that today," said Drought, "but by tomorrow there will be no well here. It shall die tonight."

"But is this not one of the sacred wells that never run dry? If not, how did it get its name?"

"I know it's sacred," said Drought, "but what good will that do? The three wise men are in paradise."

The three travellers exchanged glances. "Do you really know the history of this ancient well?" they asked.

"I know the history of all wells and fountains and brooks and rivers," said Drought with pride.

"Then grant us a pleasure, and tell us the story!" begged the strangers, and they sat down around the old enemy to living things, and listened.

Drought shook himself and crawled up on the well's rim, like a storyteller upon his improvised throne, and began his tale…

"In Gebas in Media, a city which lies near the border of the desert – so often a favourite of mine – there lived many, many years ago, three men who were famed for their wisdom.

"They were also very poor, which was most uncommon; because in Gebas knowledge was highly valued and rewarded. With these men, however, it could hardly have been otherwise because one of them was very old, one suffered from leprosy and the third was an Ethiopian. People thought the first was much too old to teach them anything; they avoided the second for fear of contagion; and they wouldn't listen to the third because they believed that no wisdom had ever come from Ethiopia.

"Meanwhile, the three wise ones became united through their common misery. They begged during the day at the same temple gate, and at night they slept on the same roof. So at least they could while away the hours together, thinking about all the wonderful things they observed in nature and in the human race.

"One night, as they slept side by side on a roof that was overgrown with red poppies, the eldest awoke. He had hardly glanced around him before he woke the other two. 'Praised be our poverty, which forces us to sleep in the open!' he said to them. 'Wake up and raise your eyes to heaven!'"

"Well," said Drought in a softer tone, "this was a night which no one who witnessed it can ever forget! The skies were so bright that the heavens looked deep and transparent and full of waves, like a sea. Light surged backwards and forwards and stars swam at varying depths: some in among the light-waves; others upon the surface.

"But farthest away and highest up, the three men saw a faint shadow appear. This shadow travelled through space like a ball, came nearer and nearer and, as it approached, began to brighten. But it brightened as roses do when they burst from their buds – may God let them all wither! It grew bigger and bigger, the dark cover around it shrank back, and light broke forth on its sides into four distinct leaves. Finally, when it had descended to the nearest of the stars, it came to a standstill. Then the dark lobes uncurled themselves back and unfolded leaf upon leaf of beautiful, shimmering, rose-coloured light, until it was perfect, and shone like a star among the stars.

"When the poor men saw this, their wisdom told them that at this moment a mighty king had been born on earth; one whose majesty and power should be greater than that of Cyrus or of Alexander. They said to one another, 'Let us go to the father and mother of the newborn baby and tell them what we've seen! Maybe they'll reward us with a purse of coins or a gold bracelet.'

"They picked up their long travelling staffs and left. They wandered through the city and out of the city gate. They hesitated for a moment as they saw before them the great stretch of dry, smooth desert, which human beings dread. Then they saw the new star cast a narrow stream of light across the desert sand, and they wandered confidently forward with the star as their guide.

"All night long they tramped over the wide, sandy plain, and throughout the entire journey they talked about the young, newborn king, who they would find lying in a golden cradle, playing with precious stones. They whiled away the hours by talking over how they should approach his father, the king, and his mother, the queen, and tell them that the heavens had foreseen power, beauty and joy greater than Solomon's for their son. They prided themselves on the fact that God had called them to see the star. They told themselves that the parents of the newborn baby would not reward them with less than twenty purses of gold; perhaps they would be given so much gold that they would no longer be poor.

"I lay in wait on the desert like a lion," said Drought, "and intended to throw myself upon these wanderers with all the agonies of thirst, but they eluded me. All night the star had led them, and in the morning when the heavens brightened and all the other stars grew pale, it remained steady and shone in the desert, guiding them to an oasis where they found a spring and a ripe fruit tree. There they rested all day. And towards night, as they saw the star's rays border the sands, they went on.

"From the human way of looking at things," continued Drought, "it was a delightful journey. The star led them so they didn't have to suffer either hunger or thirst. It led them past sharp thistles and avoided loose, flying sand; they escaped the burning sunshine and the hot desert storms. The three wise men said repeatedly to one another, 'God is protecting us and blessing our journey. We are his messengers.'

"Then they fell into my power," said Drought. "These star-wanderers' hearts were transformed into a desert as dry as the one through which they travelled. They were filled with pride and destructive greed.

"'We are God's messengers!' repeated the three wise ones. 'The father of the newborn king cannot reward us too well, even if he gives us a caravan of camels laden with gold.'

"By and by, the star led them over the famous River Jordan and up among the hills of Judea. One night it stood still over the little city of Bethlehem, which lay upon a hilltop and shone among the olive trees.

"The three wise ones looked around for castles and towers and walls, and all the other things that belong to a royal city, but they saw no such thing. And what was worse, the star's light didn't even lead them into the city but stopped over a cave near the wayside. There, the soft light stole in through the opening and revealed a little child, who was being lulled to sleep in its mother's arms.

"Although the three men saw how the star's light circled the child's head like a crown, they remained standing outside the cave. They didn't go in to prophesy honours and kingdoms for this little one. They hurried away before they could be seen, and wandered back down the hill.

"'Have we come in search of beggars as poor as ourselves?' they said. 'Has God brought us here to mock him and predict honours for a shepherd's son? This child will never do more than tend sheep here in the valley.'"

Drought chuckled to himself and nodded to his listeners, as if to say, "Am I not right? There are drier things than the desert sands, but there is nothing more barren than the human heart."

"The three wise ones had not wandered very far before they found themselves lost; they must not have followed the star correctly," continued Drought. "They turned their gaze upward to find the star and the right road, but the star they'd followed all the way from the East had vanished."

The three strangers were fidgeting, and their faces expressed deep suffering.

"What happened next," continued Drought, "follows human people's usual way of thinking, which is perhaps a blessing. When the three wise men no longer saw the star, they understood at once that they had sinned against God.

"And it happened with them," continued Drought furiously, "just as it happens with the ground in autumn when the heavy rains begin to fall: they shook with terror, as one shakes when it thunders and lightens; their whole being softened, and humility, like green grass, sprang up in their souls.

"For three nights and days they wandered about the country, searching for the child who they would worship. But the star didn't appear to them. They grew more and more bewildered, and suffered the most overwhelming anguish and despair. On the third day they came to this well to drink. God had pardoned their sin. And, as they bent over the water, they saw in its depths the reflection of the star which had brought them from the East. Instantly they found it in the sky and it led them again to the cave in Bethlehem, where they fell upon their knees before the child and said, 'We bring you golden vessels filled with incense and precious spices. You will be the greatest king that ever lived upon earth.'

"Then the child laid his hand upon their lowered heads, and when they rose the child had given them gifts greater than a king could have granted: the old beggar was young again, the leper was cured, and the Ethiopian's wisdom was sought from then on all over the world. And legend says that each wise man became a king with his own kingdom."

Drought paused in his story, and the three strangers praised it. "You have spoken well," they said. "But it surprises me," said one of them, "that the three wise men do nothing to thank the well which showed them the star. Would they entirely forget such a great blessing?"

"Shouldn't the well last for ever," said the second stranger, "to remind people that happiness, which is lost in pride and greed, can be found again in the depths of humility?"

"Can the dead who live in paradise not show gratitude, as the living do?" said the third stranger.

As he heard this, Drought sprang up with a wild cry. He finally understood who the strangers were! He ran away like a madman, so he wouldn't have to watch the Three Wise Men call their servants to lead their camels, laden with water sacks, to the poor dying well and fill it with water which they had brought down from paradise.

Bethlehem's Children

A Roman soldier stood on guard just outside the gate to Bethlehem. He was wearing full armour and a helmet, with a short sword at his side and a long spear in his hand. He stood there all day completely still, so you could easily have thought he was made of iron. The city's people went in and out of the gate and beggars lolled in the shade under the archway; fruit vendors and wine dealers set their baskets and jugs down on the ground beside the soldier, but he barely even turned his head to look at them.

It seemed as though he wanted to say, "There is nothing to see here. What do I care about you people who barter and sell, and drive here with oil casks and wine sacks? Let me see an army prepare to meet the enemy! Let me see the excitement and struggle of horsemen charging down upon a troop of foot soldiers! Let me see brave men scaling the walls of a beleaguered city! I only have eyes for war. I long to see the Roman Eagles glisten in the air! I long for the trumpets' blast, for shining weapons, for the splash of red blood!"

Just beyond the city gate was a fine meadow, overgrown with lilies. Each day the soldier stood with his eyes turned towards this meadow, but he never thought of admiring the beautiful flowers. Sometimes he noticed that passers-by stopped to appreciate the lilies, and it amazed him to think that people would lose time to look at anything so trivial. "These people don't understand true beauty," he thought.

And as he thought this, he could no longer see the green fields and olive groves around Bethlehem, but dreamed himself away to a burning hot desert in sunny Libya. He saw a legion of soldiers march forward in a long, straight line over the yellow, trackless sand. There was no protection against the sun's piercing rays, no cooling stream, no end to the desert, and no goal in sight. He saw soldiers, exhausted by hunger and thirst, march forward with faltering steps; he saw one after another drop to the ground, overcome by the scorching heat. Nevertheless, they marched onward without a murmur, without a thought of deserting their leader and turning back.

"Now, *there* is something beautiful!" thought the soldier. "Something worth the attention of a valiant man."

Standing on guard at the same post day after day, the soldier could also watch the little children who played around him. But, as with the flowers, they didn't interest him one bit. "What is there to be happy about?" he thought when he saw people smiling as they watched the children's games. "It's strange to find such pleasure in so little."

One day the soldier saw a little boy of about three years old come out onto the meadow to play. He was a poor lad, dressed in a scant sheepskin, who played all alone. The soldier stood and watched the newcomer without realising he was doing it. At first he noticed the way the boy ran so lightly over the field that he scarcely seemed to touch the tips of the blades of grass. Later he was even more astonished. "By my sword!" he exclaimed. "This child doesn't play like the others. What is he doing?"

As the child played only a few paces away, he could see well enough how he reached out his hand to catch a bee that sat on the edge of a flower. The bee was carrying so much pollen it could hardly lift its wings to fly. He saw, to his great surprise, that the bee let itself be taken without trying to escape, and without using its sting. Then, with the bee gripped between his fingers, the boy ran over to a crack in the city wall where a swarm of bees had their home, and set the bee down. As soon as he had helped one bee, he hurried back to help another. All day long the soldier watched him catch bees and carry them home.

"This must be the silliest boy I've ever seen," thought the soldier. "Why is he helping bees that can take perfectly good care of themselves and might sting him? What kind of a man will he become – if he lives long enough?"

The child came back day after day and played in the meadow, and the soldier couldn't help marvelling at him and his games.

"It's very strange," thought the soldier. "I've stood on guard for three whole years, and so far the only interesting thing I've seen is this infant."

But he was in no way pleased about this; quite the opposite! This child reminded him of a dreadful prediction made by an old Hebrew seer, who had prophesied that a time of peace would come to the world one day. No blood would be shed for a thousand years, no wars would be waged, and people would love one another like brothers. The soldier found this thought so dreadful that a shudder passed through his body, and he gripped his spear hard, as if for support.

And now, the more the soldier saw this child playing, the more he thought of the thousand-year reign of peace. He didn't like to be reminded of anything so awful!

One day when the boy was playing among the flowers, a heavy downpour of rain came bursting through the clouds. When he noticed how big and heavy the drops were that beat down upon the sensitive lilies, the child seemed anxious for his friends. He rushed to the loveliest among them and bent its stiff stem towards the ground, so the raindrops caught the petals underneath. Then he ran to another and did the same, turning the flower cups towards the ground. And then to a third and a fourth, until all the flowers in the meadow were protected against the rainfall.

The soldier smiled to himself when he saw the boy's work. "I'm afraid the lilies won't thank him for this," he said. "Every stalk will be broken. You can't bend stiff stems like that!"

But when the rain stopped, the soldier saw the little lad hurry over to the lilies and raise them up. To his utter astonishment, the boy easily straightened the stiff stalks, and not one of them was broken or bruised. He ran from flower to flower, and soon all the rescued lilies shone beautifully in the meadow.

When the soldier saw this, he was filled with rage. "What a ridiculous child!" he thought. "What kind of man will he make if he can't even bear to see a lily destroyed? What would happen if he had to go to war? What would he do if they ordered him to burn a house filled with women and children, or to sink a ship with everyone on board?"

Again he thought of the old prophecy and began to worry. "Given the nature of this child," he thought, "perhaps this awful time is drawing near. The whole earth is already at peace. Perhaps, from now on, everyone will think like this boy: they'll be afraid to injure one another, and not even have the heart to crush a bee or a flower! No great deeds will be done, no glorious battles won, and no brilliant triumvirate will march up to the Capitol. There will be nothing left for brave men to enjoy."

And the soldier – who longed for new wars, so he could fight his way to glory and become rich and powerful – felt so exasperated with the little three-year-old that he raised his spear threateningly the next time the child ran past.

Another day the boy did something that struck the soldier as being even more pointless and thankless.

It was a fearfully hot day, and the sun beat down on the soldier's helmet and armour until he felt he was wearing a suit of fire. Any passers-by could see he was suffering terribly from the heat: his bloodshot eyes were ready to burst from their sockets, and his lips were dry and shrivelled. But as he was used to the burning heat of African deserts, he thought this a mere trifle, and it didn't occur to him to move from his post. On the contrary, he took pleasure in showing the passers-by that he was so strong and hardy he didn't need to shelter from the sun.

While he was standing there letting himself be practically boiled alive, the little boy came up to him. He knew very well that the soldier was not his friend, so he was careful not to come within reach of his spear; but now he ran up to him, watched him closely, then hurried as fast as he could towards the road. When he came back, he held both hands like a bowl, carrying a few drops of water.

"Maybe this child has taken it upon himself to run and fetch water for me," thought the soldier. "He is certainly lacking common sense. Shouldn't a Roman soldier be able to stand a little heat? Why is the boy running around helping those who require no help! I don't want his compassion. I wish he and everyone like him would go away!"

The boy walked very slowly. He held his fingers close together so that no water would be spilled. As he approached the soldier, he kept his eyes fixed anxiously on the water, so he didn't see that the man stood there frowning with a forbidding look in his eye. Then the child came up to the soldier and offered him the water.

On the way, his heavy curls had tumbled down over his forehead and eyes. He shook his head several times to get the hair out of his eyes, so that he could look up. When he succeeded at last, and became conscious of the hard expression on the soldier's face, he wasn't frightened, but stood still and begged him with a bewitching smile to taste the water. But the soldier has no intention of accepting kindness from the child, whom he regarded as his enemy. He didn't look down, but stood rigid and showed no sign that he understood what the child was offering.

The boy didn't understand that the man wanted him to go away. He smiled all the while just as confidently, raised himself on the tips of his toes, and stretched his hands as high as he could so the big soldier could reach the water more easily.

The soldier felt so insulted because a mere child wished to help him that he gripped his spear to drive the boy away.

But just at that moment, the extreme heat beat down on the soldier with such intensity that he saw red flames dance before his eyes and felt his brains melt inside his head. He feared the sun would kill him if he didn't find instant relief.

Beside himself with terror, the soldier threw his spear on the ground, seized the child with both hands, lifted him up, and drank as much as he could of the water from the boy's hands.

Only a few drops touched his tongue, but it was enough.

As soon as he had tasted the water, a delicious coolness surged through his body, and his helmet and armour stopped burning. The sun's rays had lost their deadly power. His dry lips became soft and moist again, and red flames no longer danced before his eyes.

Before he had time to realise all this, he had already put down the child, who ran back to the meadow to play. Astonished, the soldier said to himself, "What kind of water was that? It was amazing! I really should thank the child."

But, seeing as he hated the boy, he soon dismissed this idea. "He's only a child," he decided. "There's no thought behind his actions. He does only what pleases him best. Did the bees or lilies thank him? He doesn't even know he saved me."

The soldier felt, if possible, even more exasperated with the child a moment later, when he saw the commander of the Roman soldiers, who were encamped in Bethlehem, come out through the gate. "Just see what a risk I ran through that little one's rash behaviour!" he thought. "If Voltigius had come a moment earlier, he would have seen me holding a child in my arms."

Meanwhile, the commander walked up to the soldier and asked him if they might have a quiet word. He had a secret he needed to share. "If we move ten paces from the gate," replied the soldier, "no one can hear us."

"You know," said the commander, "that King Herod, time and again, has searched for a child who is growing up here in Bethlehem. His soothsayers and priests have told him that this child will take his throne. Moreover, they've predicted that the new king will bring a thousand-year reign of peace and holiness. You understand, of course, that Herod would willingly make him – harmless!"

"I understand!" said the soldier eagerly. "But that should be the easiest thing in the world."

"It would certainly be very easy," said the commander, "if the king only knew which of the children here in Bethlehem it is."

The soldier frowned. "It's a pity his soothsayers can't tell him," he said.

"But now Herod has come up with a plan to make this peaceful young prince 'harmless'," continued the commander. "He promises a handsome gift to everyone who will help him."

"Whatever Voltigius commands shall be carried out, even without money or gifts," said the soldier.

"Thank you," replied the commander. "Listen now to the king's plan! He's arranging a birthday party for his youngest son, to which he'll invite all the boys in Bethlehem aged two and three years, together with their mothers. And during this party…" He stopped suddenly, and laughed when he saw the look of disgust on the soldier's face.

"My friend," he continued, "don't worry! Herod doesn't intend to use us as nurses. Now bend your ear to my mouth, and I'll tell you his plan."

The commander whispered for a long time, and when he'd finished, he said, "I need hardly tell you that absolute secrecy is vital, or the whole plot may fail."

"You know, Voltigius, that you can rely on me," said the soldier.

When the commander had gone and the soldier was alone, he looked around for the child. He had been playing among the flowers the whole time, and the soldier caught himself thinking that, skipping around among them, the boy looked almost like a butterfly.

Suddenly he began to laugh. "At least I won't have to worry much longer about this child. He'll be invited to the birthday party this evening."

He remained at his post all day, until dusk fell and it was time to close the city gate for the night.

When this was done, he wandered through the narrow, dark streets to the splendid palace that Herod owned in Bethlehem.

In the centre of this immense palace was a large stone-paved court surrounded by buildings, which each had three open galleries, one above the other. The king had ordered that the birthday party be held on the highest of these galleries, and that it should be transformed to look like a covered walkway in a beautiful flower garden. The ceiling was hidden by creeping vines hung with thick clusters of luscious grapes, and alongside the walls and against the pillars stood small pomegranate trees, laden with ripe fruit. The floors were strewn with rose leaves, lying thick and soft like a carpet. And all along the balustrades, the cornices, the tables and the low divans, ran garlands of lustrous white lilies.

Here and there stood great marble basins, where glittering gold and silver fish swam in the clear water. Multicoloured birds from distant lands perched in the trees, and an old raven sat in a cage, chattering.

Soon children and mothers filed into the gallery as the party started. The boys were given white dresses with purple borders as they entered the palace, and wreaths of roses for their dark, curly heads. The women came in, regal in crimson and blue robes and white veils, which hung in long, loose folds from high-peaked headdresses, adorned with gold coins and chains. Some carried their children on their shoulders; others led their sons by the hand; some, whose children were afraid or shy, carried them in their arms.

The women sat down on the floor of the gallery. As soon as they'd taken their places, slaves brought in low tables spread with the finest food and wine – perfect for a king's feast – and all the happy mothers began to eat and drink.

Along the farthest wall of the gallery, and almost hidden by flower garlands and fruit trees, a double line of soldiers was stationed, in full armour. They stood perfectly still, as if they had nothing to do with the party being celebrated around them. The women couldn't help but glance over now and then, wondering why this troop of iron-clad men was there.

"Why are they needed here?" they whispered. "Does Herod think we women don't know how to behave? Does he think we need so many soldiers to guard us?"

But others whispered that this was how it should be in a king's home. Herod never gave a banquet without having a house full of soldiers. The heavily armoured warriors stood there on guard to honour them.

During the first few moments of the feast, the children felt shy and uncertain, and sat quietly beside their mothers. But they soon began to run around and enjoy all the treats Herod had provided.

The king had created an enchanted land for his little guests. When they wandered through the gallery, they found beehives whose honey they could take without being stung by grumpy bees. They found bending trees which lowered their fruit-laden branches for them. In one corner they found magicians who could conjure up pockets full of toys in an instant. In another corner they discovered a wild-beast tamer, who showed them a pair of tigers so tame that they could ride them.

But nothing in this paradise of treasures attracted the boys' attention quite like the long line of soldiers who stood still as statues at the far end of the gallery. They were captivated by the soldiers' shining helmets, their stern, haughty faces and their short swords, encased in richly jewelled sheaths.

As they all played together, they couldn't stop thinking about the soldiers. They kept their distance, but they longed to get closer to the men, to see if they were really alive. To the little boys, it seemed incredible that people could stand so near the clusters of grapes and other delicacies without reaching out a hand to take them.

Finally, there was one boy who couldn't resist any longer. Slowly and cautiously he approached one of the armoured men; and when the soldier remained just as rigid and still, the child came nearer and nearer. At last the boy was so close that he could touch the soldier's shoe straps and shins.

Then – as though this childish act were a terrible crime – the iron men threw themselves in motion and seized the children angrily. Some swung boys over their heads between the lamps and garlands, over the balcony and down into the courtyard far below, where they were killed on the hard stone pavement. Others drew their swords and pierced the children's hearts. Others crushed the boys' heads against the walls before throwing them down into the dark courtyard.

At first there was an ominous stillness; the women were petrified with amazement. But as the mothers began to understand what had happened, they rushed towards the soldiers with one great cry. There were still a few children left up in the gallery who hadn't been captured during the first attack. The soldiers chased them, and their mothers threw themselves in front of them, clutching at swords with their naked hands to protect their children. Several women whose sons were already dead threw themselves upon the soldiers, trying to strangle them in revenge.

During this wild confusion, while fearful shrieks rang through the palace and the most inhuman cruelties were taking place, the soldier who guarded the city gate stood still at the top of the stairs which led down from the gallery. He took no part in the murders; he only raised his sword to the women who had managed to snatch their children and were trying to escape down the stairs. Just the sight of him, stern and stiff, was so terrifying that they flung themselves over the balcony or turned back into the heat of the struggle instead of trying to pass him.

"Voltigius certainly did the right thing when he gave me this post," thought the soldier. "A young and careless warrior would have left his position and rushed into the confusion. If I'd let myself be tempted away from here, at least ten children would have escaped."

While he was thinking this, a young woman who had snatched up her child and managed to get past all the other soldiers came rushing towards him.

"Ah, this one's about to escape!" thought the soldier. "Neither she nor the child is wounded."

The woman came towards him so quickly she appeared to be flying, and he didn't have time to catch a glimpse of her face, or that of her son. He just raised his sword, and the woman with the child in her arms was dashed against it. He expected them both to fall to the ground.

But just then the soldier heard an angry buzzing over his head, and the next instant he felt a sharp pain in one eye. It was so intense that he was stunned, bewildered, and the sword dropped from his hand. He raised his hand to his eye and caught hold of a bee. Quick as a flash, he stooped down, picked up the sword and tried to intercept the runaways.

But the little bee had done its work very well.

During the short time that the soldier was blinded, the young mother had managed to rush past him and down the stairs. And although he hurried straight after her, he couldn't find her. She'd vanished, and no one in the entire palace could find her.

The following morning, the soldier and several of his comrades stood on guard just inside the city gate. It was early and the gates had only just been opened. But this morning no crowds of field labourers streamed out of the city, as they usually did. The people of Bethlehem were so terrified after the night's bloodshed that they didn't dare to leave their homes.

"By my sword!" said the soldier, as he stood and stared down the narrow street which led towards the gate. "I think Voltigius has made a mistake. It would have been better to keep the gates closed and order a thorough search of every house in the city until he'd found the boy who escaped from the feast. Voltigius thinks his parents will try to flee when they hear that the gates are open. I don't think this is wise; it would be so easy to smuggle out a child."

He wondered if they would try to hide the boy in a fruit basket, a huge oil cask or among bales of grain.

While he stood there on the lookout for anything suspicious, a man and a woman came hurrying down the street, casting anxious looks behind them. The man gripped an axe firmly, as if determined to fight should anyone bar his way. But the soldier was more interested in the woman. She was as tall as the young mother who'd got away from him the night before. He noticed that she'd thrown her skirt over her head. "Perhaps she's doing that to cover the child in her arms," he wondered.

The closer they got, the clearer he could see the child who the woman carried under her raised robe. "I'm positive it's the one who got away last night. I didn't see her face, but I recognise her tall figure. And here she comes now with a child in her arms, and without trying very hard to keep him hidden. I hadn't dared to hope for such a lucky chance," said the soldier to himself.

The man and woman rushed up to the city gate, where they clearly hadn't expected to be stopped. They trembled with fright when the soldier levelled his spear at them and barred their passage.

"Why do you refuse to let us go to work in the fields?" asked the man.

"You may go presently," said the soldier, "but first I must see what your wife has hidden behind her robe."

"What is there to see?" said the man. "It's only bread and wine for us to eat."

"You speak the truth, perhaps," said the soldier, "but if that's true, why does she turn away? Why doesn't she willingly let me see what she carries?"

"I don't want you to see it," said the man, "and I command you to let us pass!"

With this he raised his axe, but the woman laid her hand on his arm.

"Please don't fight!" she pleaded. "I'll let him see what I'm carrying, and I know that he can't harm it." With a proud and confident smile, she turned towards the soldier and threw back a fold of her robe.

Instantly the soldier staggered back in a daze and closed his eyes. At first he didn't know what he saw; whatever the woman was carrying reflected such a dazzling white light.

"I thought you were carrying a child," he said.

"You see what I hold," the woman answered.

Then the soldier finally realised that it was only a cluster of white lilies, the same kind that grew in the meadow, but their lustre was much richer and more radiant. He could hardly bear to look at them.

He thrust his hand in among the flowers – he couldn't help thinking that a child must be hidden in there – but he felt only the cool flower petals.

He was so angry, he would gladly have taken both the man and woman prisoner, but he knew that he could give no reason for doing so.

When the woman saw his confusion, she said, "Will you let us go now?"

The soldier quietly lowered the spear and stepped aside.

The woman drew her robe over the flowers once more, smiling down sweetly at them. "I knew you couldn't harm it if you saw it," she said to the soldier.

With this, they ran off, and the soldier stood and stared after them as long as they were within sight.

While he watched them, he felt almost sure that the woman was carrying an actual, living child, not a bunch of lilies.

Then he heard loud shouts from the street. It was Voltigius with several of his men, who came running.

"Stop them!" they cried. "Close the gates on them! Don't let them escape!"

And when they reached the soldier, they said that they'd tracked the runaway boy. They had found him at home, but then he'd escaped again. They had seen his parents hurry away with him. The father was a strong, grey-bearded man who carried an axe; the mother was a tall woman who held a child concealed under a raised robe.

As Voltigius explained, a Bedouin came riding in through the gate on a good horse. Without a word, the soldier rushed up to the rider, jerked him down off the horse, threw him to the ground and, with one bound, jumped into the saddle and dashed away towards the road.

Two days later, the soldier rode onwards through the dreary mountainous desert which forms the southern part of Judea. He was still pursuing the three fugitives from Bethlehem, and he was beside himself with rage because his fruitless hunt seemed as if it would never end.

"It looks, indeed, as if they've been swallowed up by the earth," he grumbled. "How many times these last few days have I been almost within a spear's throw, and yet they've escaped me! I'm beginning to think I'll never catch them."

He felt despondent, as if he were struggling against some superior power. He wondered if the gods were protecting these people.

"This trouble is in vain. I should turn back before I die of hunger and thirst in this barren land!" he said to himself again and again. Then he was seized with fear of what awaited him at home should he turn back without having accomplished his mission.

Twice he had let the child escape, and neither Voltigius nor Herod would pardon him.

"As long as Herod knows that one of Bethlehem's children still lives, he will be haunted by the same anxiety and dread," said the soldier. "He'll probably try to ease his worries by nailing me to a cross."

The heat of midday was torturous, as he rode through the mountains on a road which wound around steep cliffs where no breeze stirred. Both horse and rider were ready to drop.

He'd lost any trace of the fugitives several hours before, and he felt more disheartened than ever.

"I must give up," he thought. "I truly believe it's a waste of time to pursue them further. They'll surely die anyway in this awful wilderness."

As he thought this, he discovered the vaulted entrance to a cave in a mountain wall near the roadside.

Immediately he rode up to the opening. "I'll rest a while in this cool mountain cave," he thought. "Then maybe I can regain the strength to keep going."

As he was about to enter, he was struck with amazement! On each side of the cave's opening grew a beautiful lily. The two stems stood there tall and erect and full of blossoms. They gave off the intoxicating scent of honey, and many bees buzzed around them.

It was such a rare sight in this wilderness that the soldier did something extraordinary. He broke off a large white flower and took it with him into the cave.

The cave was neither deep nor dark, and as soon as he entered he saw that there were already three travellers inside: a man, a woman and a child, who lay stretched out on the ground, lost in a deep sleep.

The soldier had never before felt his heart beat as it did at this sight. They were the three runaways who he'd been hunting for so long. He recognised them instantly. And here they lay sleeping, unable to defend themselves and wholly in his power.

He drew his sword quickly and bent over the sleeping child.

Cautiously he lowered the sword towards the infant's heart, and measured carefully in order to kill with a single thrust.

He paused briefly to look at the boy's face. Now, when he was certain of victory, he felt a grim pleasure in observing his victim.

But when he saw the child, his joy increased, for he recognised the little boy he'd seen playing with the bees and lilies in the meadow by the city gate.

"Why, of course, I should have known this all the time!" he thought. "This is why I've always hated the child. This is the prophesied Prince of Peace."

He lowered his sword again while he thought. "When I lay this child's head at Herod's feet he will make me Commander of his Life Guard."

As he brought the point of the sword nearer and nearer to the sleeping child's heart, he revelled in the thought. "This time at least no one will come between us and snatch him from my power."

But the soldier still held the lily that he'd picked at the cave entrance; and while he was thinking of his good fortune, a bee that had been hidden in its petals flew towards him and buzzed around his head.

He staggered back. Suddenly he remembered the bees the

boy had carried to their home, and he remembered that a bee
had helped the child escape from Herod's feast. He held the
sword suspended, and stood still and listened for the bee.

He no longer heard the tiny creature's buzzing. As he stood
there perfectly still, he became conscious of the strong, delicious
perfume coming from the lily that he held in his hand. And he
began to think of the lilies that the little one had protected from
the rain. He remembered that a cluster of lilies had hidden the
child as they escaped through the city gate.

He became more and more thoughtful, and he drew back his
sword.

"The bees and the lilies have repaid his good deeds," he

whispered to himself. Then he remembered that the boy had once been kind to him, and his face flushed a deep crimson.

"Can a Roman soldier forget to repay help that he's accepted?" he whispered.

He fought a short battle with himself. He thought of Herod and of his own desire to destroy the young Prince of Peace.

"It's not right to murder this child who has saved my life," he said at last.

And he bent down and laid his sword beside the boy, so that when they woke the fugitives would understand the danger they'd escaped.

Then he noticed that the child was awake. He lay watching the soldier with beautiful eyes that shone like stars.

And the warrior bent down on his knees in front of the child.

"Lord, you are the mighty one!" he said. "You are the strong conqueror! You are the one whom the gods love! You are the one who shall tread upon adders and scorpions!"

He kissed the boy's feet and stole softly out of the cave, while the little one smiled and smiled after him with the great, astonished eyes of a child.

The Flight into Egypt

Far away in one of the Eastern deserts many, many years ago, there grew a palm tree, which was both exceedingly old and exceedingly tall.

Everyone who passed through the desert stopped to look at it because it was much larger than other palm trees. They used to say that one day it would be taller than the obelisks and pyramids.

One day as the huge palm tree stood alone looking out over the desert, it saw something which made its mighty crown of leaves sway back and forth with astonishment on its slender trunk. Over by the desert borders walked two people. They were still at the distance at which camels seem as tiny as moths, but they were certainly two people – who were strangers in the desert, as the palm tree knew all the desert folk. They were a man and a woman, without pack camels, a tent or a water sack.

"Truly," said the palm to itself, "these two have come here to meet certain death."

The palm tree cast a quick, apprehensive glance around.

"It surprises me," it said, "that the lions are not already out to hunt this prey, but I don't see a single one stir; nor do I see any of the desert robbers, but they'll probably come soon."

"A sevenfold death awaits these travellers," thought the palm tree. "The lions will devour them, thirst will parch them, sandstorms will bury them, robbers will trap them, sunstroke will blight them and fear will destroy them." And the palm tried to think of something else, but the fate of these people made it feel sad.

On the whole desert plain that lay spread out beneath the palm, there wasn't anything which it hadn't known and observed for a thousand years. Nothing else came to mind. Again it started to think about the two wanderers.

"By the drought and the storm!" said the palm, calling upon life's most dangerous enemies. "What is the woman carrying in her arms? I believe these fools have a little child with them!"

The palm – who was long-sighted, as the old usually are – was right. The woman was holding a child, who leaned against her shoulder and slept.

"The child hasn't even got suitable clothes on," said the palm. "The mother has just tucked up her skirt and thrown it over him. She must have snatched him from his bed in great haste and rushed away. I understand now: these people are runaways.

"But they are fools, nevertheless," continued the palm. "Unless an angel protects them, they would have done better to let their enemies do their worst than to venture into this wilderness.

"I can imagine how the whole thing came about. The man stood at his work; the child slept in his crib; the woman had gone out to fetch water. When she was a few steps from the door, she saw enemies coming. She rushed back to the house, snatched up her child and fled.

"Since then, they've been on the run for several days. It's clear that they haven't rested for a moment. Yes, that's what happened, but still I say that unless an angel protects them...

"They're so frightened that, as yet, they don't feel their fatigue or pain. But I see their thirst from the strange gleam in their eyes. Surely I ought to know a thirsty person's face!"

And when the palm began to think of thirst, a shudder passed through its tall trunk, and the many lobes on its long leaves rolled up, as though they'd been held over a fire.

"If I were a human being," it said, "I would never venture into the desert. Anyone who dares come here without having roots that reach far down to the never-dying water table below is very brave. Here it can be dangerous even for palms; yes, even for a palm tree like me.

"If I could advise them, I'd beg them to turn back. Their enemies could never be as cruel towards them as the desert.

Perhaps they think it's easy to live in the desert! But I know that, now and then, even I've found it hard to stay alive. I remember one time in my youth when a hurricane threw a whole mountain of sand over me. I nearly choked."

The palm continued to think aloud, as people on their own often do.

"I can hear a wonderfully beautiful melody rushing through my leaves," it said. "All the lobes on my leaves are quivering. I don't know what's possessed me while I've been watching these poor strangers, but this unfortunate woman is so beautiful! She reminds me of the most wonderful thing I ever experienced."

And while its leaves continued to move in a soft melody, the palm was reminded how once, very long ago, two illustrious people had visited the oasis. They were the Queen of Sheba and Solomon the Wise. The beautiful queen was returning to her own country; the king had accompanied her on the journey, and now they were going to part. "In remembrance of this hour," the queen had said, "I plant a date seed in the earth, and I wish a palm will spring from it that will grow and live until a greater king than Solomon rises to the throne of Judea." And when she had said this, she planted the seed in the earth and watered it with her tears.

"I wonder why I remembered this today?" said the palm. "Can this woman be so beautiful that she reminds me of the most glorious of queens – the queen by whose word I have lived and flourished until this day?

"I hear my leaves rustle louder and louder," said the palm, "and it sounds so melancholy – as if they were predicting my life would soon end. It's good to know that it can't be true, because I can't die."

The palm assumed that the death-rustle in its leaves must be meant for the lone wanderers. They also believed that they were on the verge of death: it could be seen in their faces as they walked past the skeleton of a camel that lay in their path; it could be seen in the glances they cast back at a pair of passing vultures. There was no alternative: they were going to die!

They had caught sight of the palm and the oasis, and rushed over to find water. But when they arrived at last, they collapsed in despair because the well was dry. The woman, worn out, lay the child down, sat on the edge of the well and wept. The man flung himself down beside her and beat upon the dry earth with his fists. The palm heard how they talked about their inevitable death, and how King Herod had ordered the slaughter of all boys aged two and three because he feared that the long-awaited King of the Jews had been born.

"It rustles louder and louder in my leaves," said the palm. "These poor fugitives will soon see their last moment."

It also observed that they were terrified of the desert. The man said it would have been better if they'd stayed at home to fight the soldiers than to come here. He said they would have met an easier death.

"God will help us," said the woman.

"We are alone among beasts of prey and serpents," said the man. "We have no food and no water. How will God be able to help us?" He tore at his clothes in despair and pressed his face against the dry earth. He was hopeless, like a man with a fatal wound to the heart.

The woman stood up, but the looks she cast towards the desert spoke of hopelessness beyond bounds.

The palm heard the melancholy rustle in its leaves growing louder and louder. The woman must have heard it too, because she looked up towards the palm crowns. Suddenly she raised her arms.

"Oh, dates, dates!" she cried. There was such intense agony in her voice that the old palm wished it were as short as a broom, and the dates as easy to reach as buds on a rose bush. It knew that its crown was full of date clusters, but how could a person reach such a height?

The man had already realised that the date clusters were out of reach. He didn't even raise his head. He begged his wife not to long for the impossible.

But the child, who had been toddling about by himself

playing with sticks and straws, had heard his mother's cry. The instant she said dates, he began to stare at the tree. He thought long and hard about how he could pick the dates. His forehead was almost drawn into wrinkles under the dark curls. At last a smile stole over his face. He had found a way.

He went up to the palm, stroked it with his little hand, and said in a sweet, childish voice, "Palm, bend down! Palm, bend down!"

The palm's leaves rustled as if a hurricane had passed through them, and shudder after shudder travelled up and down its long trunk. The tree understood that this little child was its superior. It couldn't resist him.

And it bowed its long trunk before the child, as people bow before princes. In a great bow it bent itself towards the ground, and finally it came down so far that the big crown with its trembling leaves swept the desert sand.

The child didn't seem to be frightened or surprised. He laughed happily as he loosened cluster after cluster of dates from the old palm's crown. When he had plucked enough dates and the tree still lay on the ground, the child came back and stoked it and said in the gentlest voice, "Palm, stand up! Palm, stand up!"

Slowly and reverently the big tree raised itself on its slender trunk, while the leaves played like harps.

"Now I know who they're playing the death melody for," said the palm to itself when it stood erect once more. "It isn't for any of these people."

The man and the woman sank to their knees and thanked God. "You have seen our agony and cured it. You are so powerful you can bend a palm trunk like a reed. What enemy should we fear when your strength protects us?"

The next time a caravan passed through the desert, the travellers saw that the great palm's crown of leaves had withered.

"How can this be?" one of them said. "This palm couldn't die until it had seen a king greater than Solomon."

"Maybe it has seen him," another of the desert travellers answered.

In Nazareth

Once, when Jesus was only five years old, he sat on the doorstep outside his father's workshop in Nazareth, and made clay cuckoos from a lump of clay which the potter across the way had given him.

He was happier than usual. All the children in the quarter had told Jesus that the potter was a grumpy man, who couldn't be softened by smiles and kind words, so Jesus had never dared ask him for anything. He hardly knew how it had come about. He had only stood on his doorstep and looked yearningly over at his neighbour, who was casting his moulds. The next thing he knew, the potter had come over from his stall and given Jesus enough clay to make a whole wine jug.

Judas sat in the porch of the next house, his face covered with bruises and his clothes full of holes from fighting with street urchins. He was quiet for now; he neither quarrelled nor fought, but worked with a bit of clay, just as Jesus did. He hadn't managed to get this clay for himself. He hardly dared venture within sight of the potter, who complained that Judas threw stones at his fragile pots, and would have driven him away with a good beating. Jesus had shared his portion of clay with Judas.

When the two children had finished their clay cuckoos, they stood the birds in a ring. They had big, round lumps to stand on in place of feet, short tails, no necks and barely any wings. But there was a clear difference in the work of the little playmates. Judas' birds were so crooked that they kept falling over, and no matter how hard he worked with his clumsy little fingers, he couldn't make their bodies neat and well formed. Now and then he glanced slyly at Jesus to see how he managed to make his birds as smooth and even as the oak leaves in the forests on Mount Tabor.

As bird after bird was finished, Jesus became happier and happier. Each looked more beautiful to him than the last, and he regarded them all with pride and affection. They were to be his playmates, his little brothers. They would sleep in his bed, keep him company and sing to him when his mother was away. Never before had he felt so rich; never again would he feel alone.

The big strong water-carrier came walking along, and right behind him came the greengrocer, who balanced on his donkey between large empty willow baskets. The water-carrier laid his hand on Jesus' curly head and asked him about his birds. Jesus told him that they had names and could sing. All the little birds had come to him from foreign lands and told him secrets. And Jesus spoke in such a way that both the water-carrier and the greengrocer forgot about their tasks for a full hour and listened to him.

But when they wished to get on their way, Jesus pointed to Judas. "See what pretty birds Judas makes!" he said.

The greengrocer good-naturedly stopped his donkey and asked Judas if his birds also had names and could sing. But Judas knew nothing of this. He was stubbornly silent and didn't even raise his eyes from his work, so the greengrocer kicked one of his birds angrily and rode on.

And so the afternoon passed, and the sun sank so far down that its beams shone through the low city gate, which stood at the end of the street and was decorated with a Roman Eagle. The sunshine that came at the close of the day was perfectly rose-red – as if it had been mixed with blood – and it coloured everything that fell in its path as it filtered through the narrow street. It painted the potter's vessels, as well as the log that creaked under the woodman's saw and the white veil that covered Mary's face.

But the loveliest of all was the sun's reflection in the little puddles that had gathered in the big, uneven cracks in the stones that covered the street. Suddenly Jesus stuck his hand in the puddle nearest to him. He imagined that he could paint his grey birds with the sparkling sunbeams that had given such pretty colour to the water, the house walls and everything around him.

The sunshine took pleasure in letting itself be captured like paint in a paint pot, and when Jesus spread it over the little clay birds, it lay still and coated them from head to feet with a diamond sheen.

Judas, who every now and then looked at Jesus to see if he made prettier birds than he did, gave a shriek of delight when he saw how Jesus painted his clay cuckoos with the sunshine from the puddles. Judas also dipped his hand in the shining water and tried to catch the sunshine.

But the sunshine wouldn't be caught by him. It slipped through his fingers, and no matter how fast he tried to move his hands to get hold of it, it got away. He couldn't catch even a pinch of colour for his poor birds.

"Wait, Judas!" said Jesus. "I'll come and paint your birds."

"No, don't touch them!" cried Judas. "They're good enough as they are."

He stood up, his eyebrows contracted into an ugly frown, his lips puckering. And he put his broad foot on the birds and squashed them, one after another, into little flat pieces of clay.

When all his birds were destroyed, he walked over to Jesus, who sat stroking his glittering jewel-like birds. Judas looked at them for a moment in silence, then he raised his foot and crushed one of them.

When Judas took his foot away and saw the little bird stamped into a cake of clay, he felt so relieved that he began to laugh, and he raised his foot to crush another.

"Judas," said Jesus, "what are you doing? Don't you see that they're alive and can sing?"

But Judas laughed and crushed yet another bird.

Jesus looked around for help. Judas was bigger than Jesus, and he wasn't strong enough to hold him back. Jesus glanced

51

around for his mother. She wasn't far away, but Judas would have had plenty of time to destroy the birds before she got back.

Tears sprang to Jesus' eyes. Judas had already crushed four of his birds. There were only three left. He was annoyed with his birds, which stood so calmly and let themselves be trampled on without noticing they were in danger. Jesus clapped his hands to awaken them, then he shouted, "Fly, fly!"

The three birds began to move their tiny wings and, fluttering anxiously, they managed to swing themselves up to the eaves of the house where they were safe.

But when Judas realised that the birds flew at Jesus' command, he began to weep. He tore his hair, as he'd seen his elders do when they were in great trouble, and he threw himself at Jesus' feet.

Judas lay there and rolled in the dust before Jesus like a dog, and kissed his feet and begged that he would raise his foot and crush him, as he had done with the clay cuckoos. Judas loved Jesus. He admired and worshipped him, but at the same time hated him.

Mary, who sat all the while watching the children play, came up and lifted Judas in her arms. She sat him on her lap and comforted him.

"You poor child!" she said to him. "You're trying to do something that no mortal man can achieve. How can any of us compete with someone who can paint with sunbeams and blow the breath of life into dead clay? If you want to be happy, don't try to compete again."

In the Temple

Once there was a poor family – a man, his wife and their son – who were visiting the big temple in Jerusalem. The son was such a beautiful child! His hair fell in long, even curls, and his eyes shone like stars.

The son hadn't been to the temple since he was big enough to understand what he saw, and now his parents had decided to show him all its treasures. There were long rows of pillars and gilded altars; there were holy men who sat and taught their pupils; there was the high priest with his breastplate of precious stones. There were the curtains from Babylon, interwoven with gold roses; there were the great copper gates, which were so heavy that it was hard work for thirty men to swing them back and forth on their hinges.

But the boy, who was only twelve years old, didn't care very much about seeing all this. His mother told him that these were the most marvellous things in the whole world. She told him that it would probably be a long time before he would see anything like it again. In the poor town of Nazareth, where they lived, there was nothing to see but dull streets.

Her praise of the magnificent temple didn't mean anything to the boy; he looked as though he would have happily run back to Nazareth to play in the narrow streets.

But it was also clear that the more indifferent the boy appeared, the more pleased his parent became. They nodded to each other over his head and were thoroughly satisfied.

At last, the child looked so tired and bored that the mother felt sorry for him. "We have walked too far with you," she said. "Come, let's rest for a while."

She sat down beside a pillar and told him to lie down on the ground with his head on her knee. He did so, and instantly fell asleep.

He had barely closed his eyes when the wife said to the husband, "I've never feared anything so much as the moment we came here to Jerusalem's temple. I thought when he saw this house of God, he'd want to stay here for ever."

"I've been dreading this journey too," said the man. "When he was born, so many signs and wonders suggested that he would become a great ruler. But what could royal honours bring him except worry and danger? I've always said it would be best, both for him and for us, if he never became anything but a carpenter in Nazareth."

"No miracles have happened around him since he was five years old," said his mother reflectively, "and he doesn't remember any of the miracles from his early childhood. Now he's just like a child among other children. God's will be done above all else! But I've almost begun to hope that our Lord in his mercy will choose another to perform great deeds, and let me keep my son."

"I'm certain," said the man, "that if he isn't told about the signs and wonders of his first years, then all will go well."

"I never speak to him about them," said the wife. "But I'm still afraid that something beyond my control will make him understand who he is. Bringing him to this temple was what I feared most."

"Let's be glad that the danger is over now," said the man. "We'll soon have him back home in Nazareth."

"I've feared the wise men in the temple," said the woman. "I've dreaded the soothsayers who sit here on their rugs. I believed that when they recognised him, they would bow before him and greet him as Judea's king. It's strange that they don't notice his beauty. They must have never seen a child like him."

She sat in silence a moment and looked at her son. "I can hardly understand it," she said. "I thought when he saw the judges who sit in the temple and settle people's disputes, and these teachers who talk with their pupils, and these priests who serve the Lord, he would wake up and say, 'It's here, among these judges, these teachers, these priests, that I was born to live.'"

"What happiness would there be for him to sit shut in between these pillars?" said the man. "It's better for him to roam on the hills and mountains around Nazareth."

The mother sighed a little. "He's so happy at home with us!" she said. "How contented he seems when he follows the shepherds on their lonely wanderings, or when he goes out in the fields to watch the labourers. It can't be wrong for us to want to keep him for ourselves."

"We only want to spare him from suffering," said the man.

They continued talking like this until the boy woke up.

"Well," said the mother, "have you had a good rest? Stand up now. Evening is drawing in and we must return to the camp."

They were in the most remote part of the building, so they began to walk towards the entrance.

They had to go through an old arch which had been there ever since the first temple was erected on this spot. Near the arch, propped against a wall, stood an old copper trumpet, enormous in length and weight, almost like lifting a pillar to play on. It was dented and battered, full of dust and spiders' webs inside and out, and covered with an almost invisible tracing of ancient letters. A thousand years had probably gone by since anyone had tried to make a sound out of it.

But when the boy saw the huge trumpet, he stopped, astonished! "What's that?" he asked.

"That's the great trumpet called the Voice of the Prince of this World," replied the mother. "With this, Moses called together the Children of Israel when they were scattered over the wilderness. Since his time no one has been able to coax a single sound from it. But the person who can will rule over all the people on earth."

She smiled at this, which she believed to be an old myth, but the boy remained standing beside the big trumpet until she called him. This trumpet was the first thing he'd seen in the temple that he liked.

They hadn't gone far before they came to a wide court. Here, in the mountain-foundation itself, was a deep, wide chasm, which had been there since time immemorial. King Solomon had decided not to fill this chasm in when he built the temple. No bridge had been laid over it; no enclosure had been built around the steep abyss. But instead, he'd stretched a sharp, steel sword across it, several feet long, with the blade pointing up. And after ages and ages and many changes to the temple, the sword still lay across the chasm, though by now it had almost rusted away. It was no longer securely fastened at the ends, so it trembled and rocked as soon as anyone walked with heavy steps in the temple court.

When the mother guided the boy around the chasm, he asked, "What bridge is this?"

"It was placed there by King Solomon," she replied, "and we call it Paradise Bridge. If you can cross the chasm on this trembling bridge, with a surface thinner than a sunbeam, you can be sure of getting to paradise."

She smiled and moved away, but the boy stood still and looked at the narrow, trembling steel blade until she called him.

When he obeyed her, she sighed with relief. She hadn't shown him these two remarkable things sooner, so he wouldn't have enough time to look at them properly.

Now they walked on without stopping until they came to the great entrance portico with its columns, five deep. Here in a corner were two black marble pillars built on the same foundation, and so close to each other that hardly a straw could be squeezed in between them. They were tall and majestic, with capitals richly decorated by a row of peculiar beasts' heads. And there wasn't an inch on these beautiful pillars that wasn't covered with marks and scratches. They were worn and damaged like nothing else in the temple. Even the floor around them had been worn smooth and hollowed out from the wear of many feet.

Once more the boy stopped his mother and asked, "What pillars are these?"

"Our father Abraham brought these pillars with him to Palestine from faraway Chaldea, and he called them Righteousness' Gate. The person who can squeeze between them is righteous before God and has never committed a sin."

The boy stood still and regarded these pillars with great big, open eyes.

"Surely you're not going to try and squeeze yourself between them?" laughed the mother. "You can see how the floor around them has been worn away by everyone who has attempted to force their way through the narrow space; but, believe me, no one has succeeded. Let's hurry! I can hear the copper gates clanging. The thirty temple servants are pushing them closed."

But that night the boy lay awake in the tent, thinking about nothing but Righteousness' Gate and Paradise Bridge and the Voice of the Prince of this World. Never before had he heard of such wonderful things, and he couldn't get them out of his head.

The following morning he still couldn't think of anything else. That morning they were leaving to go home. The boy's parents had a lot to do before they took the tent down and loaded it on a big camel, and before everything else was in order. They weren't travelling alone, but with many relatives and neighbours. And since there were so many, the packing naturally took a long time.

The boy wasn't helping. In the midst of the hurry and confusion he sat still and thought about the three wonderful things.

Suddenly he decided he had enough time to go back to the temple and take another look at them. There was still so much to be packed away. He could probably get back from the temple before it was time to leave.

He hurried away without telling anyone where he was going. He didn't think it was necessary. He would soon return, of course.

It wasn't long before he reached the temple and entered the portico where the two pillars stood.

He sat down on the floor beside them and gazed up at them. He thought how incredible it would be to squeeze in between the two pillars, and how the person who could would be righteous in the eyes of God and never have committed a sin. He believed this was the most amazing thing he'd ever heard. But they stood so close together it was impossible to even try. Without realising, he sat still by the pillars for almost an hour. He thought he'd only been there a few moments.

The judges of the high court were assembled in this portico, helping people to settle their differences. The whole place was filled with people complaining about boundary lines that had been moved, about sheep that had been stolen from flocks and branded with false marks, about debtors who wouldn't pay.

Among them came a rich man dressed in a trailing purple robe, who brought before the court a poor widow who was supposed to owe him a few silver shekels. The poor widow cried and said that the rich man had treated her unfairly; she'd already paid her debt to him once, and now he tried to force her to pay it again, but she couldn't afford to. She was so poor that if the judges condemned her to pay, she would be forced to give her daughters to the rich man as slaves.

Then the principal judge turned to the rich man and said, "Do you dare to swear on oath that this poor woman has not already paid you?"

And the rich man answered, "Lord, I am a rich man. Would I take the trouble to demand money from this poor widow if I didn't have the right to it? I swear to you that, as certain as that no one shall ever walk through Righteousness' Gate, this woman owes me the money I'm asking for."

When the judges heard this oath they believed him, and doomed the poor widow to leave him her daughters as slaves.

The boy was sitting close by and heard all this. He thought to himself, "It would be so good if someone could squeeze through Righteousness' Gate! That rich man certainly isn't telling the truth. It's such a pity about the poor old woman, who will be forced to send her daughters away as slaves!"

He jumped on the platform where the two pillars towered, and looked through the crack.

"Oh, I wish it wasn't impossible!" he thought.

He felt so sad about the poor woman. He didn't even remember the myth about the person squeezing through Righteousness' Gate being holy and without sin. He just wanted to get through for the poor woman's sake.

He put his shoulder in the groove between the two pillars, as if to make a path.

At that moment, everyone who stood under the portico looked over towards Righteousness' Gate because it rumbled in the vaults, and it sang in the old pillars, and they glided apart – one to the right, one to the left – and made a space wide enough for the boy's slender body to pass between them!

The people were so amazed that, at first, no one knew what to say. They stood and stared at the little boy who had worked such a great miracle.

The oldest judge was the first to come to his senses. He declared that they should bring the rich merchant before the judgment seat. And he sentenced him to leave all his goods to the poor widow, because he had sworn falsely in God's temple.

When this was settled, the judge asked about the boy who had passed through Righteousness' Gate, but when the people looked around for him, he'd disappeared. In the very moment the pillars glided apart, the boy had woken, as if from a dream, and remembered his parents and the journey home.

"I must hurry so my parents don't have to wait for me," he thought. He didn't realise he'd spent so long at Righteousness' Gate, and he thought he had time to look at Paradise Bridge before leaving the temple.

He slipped through the crowd of people and came to Paradise Bridge. When he saw the sharp steel sword that was drawn across the chasm, and thought how the person who could walk across that bridge was sure of reaching paradise, he believed this was the most marvellous thing he'd ever heard. He sat down on the edge of the chasm to look at the steel sword. He thought

how delightful it would be to reach paradise, and how much he would like to walk across the bridge, but at the same time he realised it would be impossible to even attempt it.

So he sat and mused for two hours, but he didn't realise how the time had flown by. He sat there and thought only of paradise.

A large altar had been built in this court, and white-robed priests walked around it, tending the altar fire and receiving sacrifices. The court was full of people with offerings and a big crowd who watched the service.

Then a poor old man came along with a small, thin lamb, which had been bitten by a dog and had a large wound.

The man took the lamb up to the priests and begged to offer it, but they refused to accept it. They told him they couldn't offer such a miserable gift to our Lord. The old man implored them to accept the lamb out of compassion, because his son lay on the verge of death, and he owned nothing else that he could offer to God to ask for his healing. "Please let me offer it," he said, "or my prayers will not reach God and my son will die!"

"You have my deepest sympathy," said the priest, "but the law forbids us to sacrifice a damaged animal. It's as impossible to grant your prayers as it is to cross Paradise Bridge."

The boy was sitting nearby, so he heard all this. Instantly he thought what a pity it was that no one could cross the bridge. Perhaps the poor man's son would survive if the lamb were sacrificed.

The old man was inconsolable as he left the temple court, but the boy got up, walked over to the trembling bridge and put his foot on it.

He didn't think at all about crossing it to be certain of paradise. He only thought of the poor man who he wanted to help. He drew back his foot and thought, "This is impossible. It's much too old and rusty, and wouldn't hold even me!"

But once again his thoughts went out to the old man whose son lay at death's door. Again he put his foot down on the blade.

Then he noticed that it had stopped trembling, and that it felt broad and secure under his foot.

And when he took the next step, he felt the air around him supporting him so he couldn't fall. It lifted him as though he were a bird with wings.

A sweet tone trembled from the suspended sword when the boy walked on it, and one of the people who stood in the court turned around to hear it. He gave a cry, and the others turned to see the little boy tripping across the sword.

There was great consternation among everyone who stood there. The first to come to their senses were the priests. They immediately sent a messenger after the poor man, and when he was brought back, they said to him, "God has performed a miracle to show us that he will accept your offering. Give us your lamb and we will sacrifice it."

When this was done they asked about the boy who had walked across the chasm, but when they looked for him they couldn't find him.

Just after the boy had crossed the chasm, he happened to think of his parents and the journey home. He didn't know that the whole morning was gone, but thought, "I must hurry and get back so they don't have to wait. But first I want to run over and take a look at the Voice of the Prince of this World." And he stole away through the crowd and ran over to the damp aisle where the copper trumpet stood leaning against the wall.

When he saw it, and thought about the prediction that the person who could make a sound from it would one day gather all the people of earth under his rule, he thought he'd never seen anything so wonderful! And he sat down beside it to look at it.

He thought how great it would be to lead all the people of earth, and how much he wanted to blow in the old trumpet. But he understood that it was impossible, so he didn't even dare try.

He sat like this for several hours, but he didn't know how the time passed. He thought only how marvellous it would be to gather all the people of earth under his rule.

In this cool passageway a holy man was teaching his pupils, who sat at his feet.

Now this holy man turned towards one of his pupils and told

him that he was an impostor. He said the spirit had revealed that this youth was a foreigner and not an Israelite. And he demanded why he'd sneaked in among his pupils under a false name.

The strange youth rose and said that he'd wandered through deserts and sailed over great seas to hear the wisdom of God. "My soul was faint with longing," he said to the holy man. "But I knew that you wouldn't teach me if I wasn't an Israelite, so I lied to you, and I pray that you'll let me stay here with you."

But the holy man stood up and raised his arms towards heaven. "It's as impossible to let you remain here with me as it is that someone will blow in the huge copper trumpet, which we call the Voice of the Prince of this World! You're not even permitted to enter this part of the temple. Leave this place at once, or my pupils will tear you to pieces, because your presence desecrates the temple."

But the youth stood still, and said, "I don't want to go elsewhere, where my soul can find no nourishment. I would rather die here at your feet."

He had hardly said this when the holy man's pupils jumped to their feet to drive him away. When he resisted them, they threw him down and tried to kill him.

But the boy was sitting nearby, so he heard and saw all this, and he thought, "This is a great injustice. If I could only blow in the big copper trumpet, he would be helped."

He stood up and laid his hand on the trumpet. At this moment he'd forgotten that blowing into it would make him a great ruler; he only hoped to help the youth whose life was in danger.

He grasped the copper trumpet with his tiny hands and tried to lift it.

Then he felt the huge trumpet raise itself to his lips. And when he breathed, a strong, resonant tone sounded from the trumpet and reverberated through the great temple.

Everyone turned their eyes and saw that a little boy stood with the trumpet at his lips and made sounds from it which shook the foundations and pillars.

Instantly, all the hands which had been lifted to strike the strange youth fell, and the holy teacher said to him, "Come and sit here at my feet as you did before! God has performed a miracle to show me that he wants you to be consecrated to his service."

As it drew on towards the close of day, a man and a woman came hurrying towards Jerusalem. They looked frightened and anxious, and called out to everyone they met, "We've lost our son! We thought he had followed our relatives, but none of them have seen him. Have any of you passed a child alone?"

Those who came from Jerusalem answered them, "We've not seen your son, but in the temple we saw a most beautiful child! He was like an angel from heaven, and he has passed through Righteousness' Gate."

They would gladly have talked in great detail about this, but the parents had no time to listen.

When they had walked on a little farther, they met other people and questioned them.

But those who came from Jerusalem only wanted to talk about a most beautiful child who looked as though he'd come down from heaven, and who had crossed Paradise Bridge.

They would gladly have stopped and talked about this until late at night, but the man and woman had no time to listen, and hurried into the city.

They walked up one street and down another without finding their son. At last they reached the temple. As they came up to it, the woman said, "Since we're here, let's go in and see what this child is like who they say has come down from heaven." They went in and asked where they could find the child.

"Go straight to where the holy teachers sit with their students. There you'll find him. The old men are questioning him and he is questioning them, and they're all amazed at him. All the people are standing below in the temple court to catch a glimpse of the boy who has raised the Voice of the Prince of this World to his lips."

The man and woman made their way through the crowd

of people, and realised that the child who sat among the wise teachers was their son.

As soon as the woman recognised him she began to weep.

And when the boy heard someone weeping, he knew it was his mother. He came over to her, and the family left the temple together.

But as the mother continued to weep, the child asked, "Why are you crying, Mother? I came as soon as I heard your voice."

"Should I not weep?" said the mother. "I thought I'd lost you."

They left the city, darkness drew in, and all the while the mother wept.

"Why are you crying?" asked the child. "I didn't know I'd been gone all day. I thought it was still morning, and I came as soon as I heard your voice."

"Should I not weep?" said the mother. "I've been looking for you all day long. I thought I'd lost you."

They walked the whole night, and all the while the mother wept.

When day began to dawn, the boy said, "Why are you crying? I wasn't looking for my own glory, but God let me perform miracles because He wanted to help the three poor people. As soon as I heard your voice, I came."

"My son," replied the mother, "I weep because you are still lost to me. You will nevermore belong to me. From now on your life's goal will be righteousness; you will long for paradise; and your love will embrace all the poor people who live on this earth."

Saint Veronica

I

Towards the end of Emperor Tiberius's reign, a poor vine-tender and his wife went to live in an isolated hut in the Sabine Mountains. They had come from a foreign land and were completely alone. They never had any visitors. But one morning when the labourer opened his door he found, to his astonishment, that an old woman sat huddled up on the doorstep. She was wrapped in a plain grey robe and looked very poor. Nevertheless, as she stood up and came to meet him, he felt a deep respect for her; she reminded him of legends about goddesses, disguised as old women, who had visited mortals.

"My friend," said the old woman, "please don't be alarmed that I slept on your doorstep last night. My parents lived in this hut, and I was born here nearly ninety years ago. I expected to find it empty and deserted. I didn't know people still lived here."

"I'm not surprised that you thought a hut which lies so high up among these desolate hills should stand empty and deserted," said the vine-tender. "But my wife and I come from a foreign land and, as poor outsiders, we haven't been able to find a better place to live. You must be tired and hungry after your long journey, especially given your age; perhaps it's better that you find the hut occupied by people than by Sabine mountain wolves. You'll at least find a bed inside to rest on and a bowl of goat's milk and bread, if you will accept them."

The old woman smiled fleetingly, but not for long enough to dispel her expression of deep sorrow.

"I spent my entire youth up here among these mountains," she said. "I haven't forgotten how to drive a wolf from his lair."

She actually looked so strong and fit that the labourer didn't doubt she could, despite her old age, fight the wild beasts of the forest.

He repeated his invitation, and the old woman stepped into the cottage. She sat down and eagerly shared the frugal meal. Although she seemed to be satisfied with the poor offering of coarse bread soaked in goat's milk, both the man and his wife thought, "Where can this old wanderer have come from? I daresay she's eaten pheasants served on silver platters more often than she's drunk goat's milk from earthen bowls."

Now and then she raised her eyes from the food and looked around, as if she were trying to remember the hut. The poor old home with its bare clay walls and earth floor certainly hadn't changed much. She pointed out to her hosts that there were still some traces of dog and deer pictures on the walls, which her father had sketched to amuse his children. And on a shelf, high up, she thought she saw fragments of an earthen dish that she herself had used to measure milk.

The man and his wife thought to themselves, "It must be true that she was born in this hut, but she's surely had more to attend to in life than milking goats and making butter and cheese."

They observed also that her thoughts were often far away, and that she sighed heavily and anxiously every time she came back to herself.

Finally she rose from the table. She thanked them graciously for the hospitality she had enjoyed, and walked towards the door.

But she seemed pitifully poor and lonely, so the vine-tender said, "If I'm not mistaken, when you dragged yourself up here last night, you'd not been planning to leave this hut so soon. If you're as poor as you seem, you must have intended to stay here for the rest of your life. But now you wish to leave because my wife and I are living here."

The old woman didn't deny that he'd guessed rightly. "But this hut, which has been deserted for many years, belongs to you as much as to me," she said. "I have no right to drive you from it."

"It's still your parents' hut," said the labourer, "and you surely have more right to it than we have. Besides, we are young and you are old, so you shall remain and we will go."

When the old woman heard this, she was astonished. She turned round on the doorstep and stared at the man as though she hadn't understood what he meant.

But now the young wife joined in the conversation. "If I might suggest," she said to her husband, "you could ask this old woman if she won't look upon us as her own children, and let us stay with her and take care of her. What good would it do to give her this miserable hut and then leave her? It would be terrible for her to live here in this wilderness alone. And what would she live on? It would be like letting her starve to death."

The old woman went up to the man and his wife and regarded them carefully. "Why do you speak like this?" she asked. "Why are you so kind to me? You are strangers."

Then the young wife answered, "Because we ourselves once met with great kindness."

II

This is how the old woman came to live in the vine-tender's hut. She became great friends with the young people. But she never told them where she had come from or who she was, and they understood that she didn't want to be asked.

One evening, when the day's work was done and all three sat on the big, flat rock which lay in front of the entrance eating their evening meal, they saw an old man coming up the path.

He was tall and powerfully built, with shoulders as broad as a gladiator's. His face wore a stern, cheerless expression. His brows jutted far out over his deep-set eyes, and the lines around his mouth expressed bitterness and contempt. He walked briskly and boldly.

The man wore a simple robe, and the instant the vine-tender saw him, he said, "He's an old soldier who's been discharged from service and is now on his way home."

When the stranger passed by them, he paused, as if in doubt. The vine-tender, who knew that the road ended a short distance beyond the hut, laid down his spoon and called out to him, "Are you lost, stranger, since you're coming this way? No one usually takes the trouble to climb up here unless he has an errand with one of us."

The stranger came nearer. "You're right," he said. "I've taken the wrong road, and now I don't know which way to go. I'd be grateful if you'd let me rest here a while, and then tell me the way to a farm."

As he spoke he sat down on one of the stones in front of the hut. The young woman asked if he'd like to share their supper, but he declined with a smile. On the other hand, he was very happy to talk with them while they ate. He asked the young folk about their way of life and their work, and they answered him frankly and cheerfully.

Suddenly the vine-tender turned towards the stranger and asked him, "You see how lonely and isolated our way of life is; it must be at least a year since I've talked with anyone except shepherds and vineyard labourers. Can you tell us something about Rome and the emperor?"

He'd hardly said this when the young wife saw the old woman give her husband a warning glance, so she raised her hand to signify, "Be careful what you say."

The stranger, meanwhile, answered very affably, "I understand that you take me for a soldier, which is not untrue, although I've long since left service. During Tiberius's reign there hasn't been much work for we soldiers. Yet he was once a great commander. Those were the days of his good fortune. Now he thinks of nothing except guarding himself against conspiracies. In Rome everyone is talking about how, last week, he let Senator Titius be taken prisoner and executed because of a mere rumour."

"The poor emperor has lost his way!" exclaimed the young woman, and shook her head in pity and surprise.

"You're absolutely right," said the stranger, as an expression of deep sorrow crossed his face. "Tiberius knows that everyone hates him, and it's driving him insane."

"What are you saying?" the woman replied. "Why should we hate him? We're only disappointed that he's no longer the great emperor he was at the beginning of his reign."

"You're mistaken," said the stranger. "Everyone detests Tiberius. Why shouldn't they? He's nothing but a cruel and merciless tyrant. The citizens of Rome think he'll become even more unreasonable from now on."

"Has anything happened, then, to make him worse than he already was?" asked the vine-tender.

When he said this, the wife noticed the old woman giving him another warning signal, but so stealthily that her husband couldn't see it.

The stranger answered him pleasantly, but at the same time a singular smile played about his lips.

"You've perhaps heard that, until now, Tiberius had a reliable friend in his household who always told him the truth. All the other people who live in his palace are fortune hunters and hypocrites, who praise the emperor's wicked acts just as much as his good ones. But there was one true friend who was never afraid to tell the emperor the truth about his actions. This person, who was more courageous than senators and generals, was the emperor's old nurse, Faustina."

"I've heard of her," said the labourer. "I gather the emperor has always been a good friend to her."

"Yes, Tiberius rewarded her affection and loyalty. He treated this poor peasant woman, who came from a miserable hut in the Sabine Mountains, as his second mother. He let her live in a mansion on the Palatine, so that she was always nearby. None of Rome's noblewomen has fared better than she. She would be carried through the streets in a litter, and she wore the clothes of an empress. When the emperor moved to Capri, she accompanied him, and he bought a country estate for her there, and filled it with slaves and lavish furniture."

"She has certainly fared well," said the husband.

He kept up the conversation with the stranger while his wife sat silent, observing the sudden change which had come over the old woman. Since the stranger arrived, she hadn't spoken a word. She had pushed her food aside, and sat up rigidly against the doorpost, staring straight ahead with a stony face.

"The emperor wanted her to live a happy life," said the stranger. "But, despite all his kindness, she too has deserted him."

The old woman gave a start at these words, but the young wife laid her hand calmly on her arm. Then she began to speak in a soft, sympathetic voice. "I can't believe that Faustina was as happy at court as you say," she said, as she turned towards the stranger. "I'm sure that she loved Tiberius as if he had been her own son. I can understand how proud she was of his noble youth, and I can understand how it must have grieved her to see him become so suspicious and cruel in his old age, especially after all her guidance and support. It must have been terrible for her to plead with him in vain, and unbearable to see him sink lower and lower."

The stranger, astonished, leaned forward a little when he heard this; but the young woman didn't glance up at him. She kept her eyes lowered, and spoke very calmly and gently.

"Perhaps you're right about the old woman," he replied. "Faustina hadn't been happy at court. It seems strange, nevertheless, that she's left the emperor now in his old age after putting up with him for her entire life."

"Has old Faustina left the emperor?" asked the husband.

"She ran away from Capri without a trace," said the stranger. "She left just as poor as she came, without taking any of her treasures."

"And doesn't the emperor know where she's gone?" asked the wife.

"No. No one knows which path she took, but they assume she's taken refuge among her native mountains."

"And the emperor doesn't know why she left?" asked the young woman.

"No, the emperor has no idea. He once accused her of serving him for money and gifts alone, like all the rest, but he can't believe she'd leave him for this. She knows deep down that he's never doubted her unselfishness. He only hopes that she'll return one day of her own accord, because she of all people knows that he has no other friends."

"I don't know Faustina," said the young woman, "but I think I can tell you why she left the emperor. The old woman was brought up among these mountains in simplicity and piety, and she has always longed to come back here again. She would never have abandoned the emperor if he hadn't insulted her. But, when he did, she felt she had the right to think of herself, since her days are numbered. If I were a poor woman of the mountains, that's what I would have done. I would have thought I'd done enough in serving my master for a whole lifetime. I would have chosen to abandon luxury and royal favours to give my soul a taste of honour and integrity before it left me for the long journey."

The stranger glanced at the young woman with a deep and tender sadness. "But now the emperor will be even more angry and cruel. Now there's no one to calm him when he's overcome with suspicion and hatred. Think of this," he continued, as he stared deeply into the young woman's eyes: "there's no one in the entire world who he doesn't hate, no one he doesn't despise – no one!"

As he uttered these words of bitter despair, the old woman moved suddenly and turned towards him, but the young woman looked him straight in the eyes and answered, "Tiberius knows Faustina will come back whenever he wants her to. But only after vice and infamy have been banished from his court."

They had all risen during this speech, but the vine-tender and his wife now stood in front of the old woman, as if to shield her.

The stranger didn't say another word, but gave the old woman a questioning glance, as if to say, "Is this your last word too?" The old woman's lips quivered, but no words came out.

"If the emperor loves his old servant, then he can let her live her last days in peace," said the young woman.

The stranger hesitated again, but suddenly his dark look brightened. "My friends," he said, "whatever we say of Tiberius, there's one thing he's learned better than others – and that is renunciation. I have only one thing more to say to you: if this old woman, Faustina, comes to this hut, treat her well. The emperor's favour rests upon anyone who helps her."

He wrapped himself up in his robe and departed the same way that he'd come.

III

After this, the vine-tender and his wife never again spoke to the old woman about the emperor. Between themselves, they marvelled that she, at her great age, had had the strength to renounce all the wealth and power she'd been accustomed to. "I wonder if she'll go back to Tiberius soon?" they asked themselves. "I'm sure she still loves him. She's left him in the hope that it will make him realise how badly he's behaving, and change for the better."

"A man as old as the emperor will never turn over a new leaf," said the labourer. "Who could teach him to love his fellow man? Until this happens, he'll keep on being cruel and suspicious of those around him."

"You know, there is someone who could do it," said the wife. "I often wonder what would happen if the two should meet. But God's ways are not our ways."

The old woman didn't seem to miss her former life at all. After a time the young wife gave birth to a child. The old woman looked after the baby, and she seemed so happy with her new role, you would have thought she'd forgotten all her sorrows.

Once every half-year she used to wrap her long, grey robe around her, and wander down to Rome. She didn't go to speak to anyone, but went straight to the Forum. Here she stopped outside a little temple on one side of the superbly decorated square.

All there was of this temple was an uncommonly large altar, which stood in a marble-paved court under the open sky. On the top of the altar, Fortuna, the goddess of happiness, was enthroned, and at its foot was a statue of Tiberius. Encircling the court were buildings for the priests, storerooms for fuel and stalls for the sacrificial beasts.

Old Faustina never journeyed further into Rome than this temple, where people came to pray for the welfare of Tiberius. When she cast a glance inside and saw that both the goddess's and the emperor's statues were wreathed in flowers; that the sacrificial fire burned; that crowds of reverent worshippers were assembled before the altar, and heard the sound of the priests' low chants, she turned around and went back to the mountains.

This is how she found out, without having to ask anyone, that Tiberius was still alive and well.

The third time she undertook this journey, she met with a surprise. When she reached the little temple, she found it empty and deserted. No fire burned in front of the statue, and there were no worshippers. A couple of dried garlands still hung on one side of the altar, but this was all that remained of its former glory. The priests were gone, and the emperor's statue, which stood there unguarded, was damaged and spattered with mud.

The old woman turned to the first passer-by. "What does this mean?" she asked. "Is Tiberius dead? Have we another emperor?"

"No," replied the Roman, "Tiberius is still emperor, but we've stopped praying for him. Our prayers can't help him any more."

"My friend," said the old woman, "I live far away among the mountains where no news reaches us. Please tell me what dreadful misfortune has happened to the emperor?"

"The most dreadful of all misfortunes! He's suffering from a disease that's never been known in Italy before, but seems to be common in the East. Since he caught it, the emperor's features have changed, his voice has become like an animal's grunt, and his toes and fingers are rotting away. And there seems to be no cure for this illness. They believe he'll die within a few weeks. But if he doesn't die, he'll lose his throne; such an ill and wretched man can no longer conduct the affairs of state. You see, his fate is sealed. It's useless to ask the gods to save him," he added, with a faint smile. "No one has anything more to either hope or fear from him, so why should we trouble ourselves on his account?"

He nodded and walked away, but the old woman stood there, stunned.

For the first time in her life she collapsed and seemed to suffer from her old age. She stood with a bent back and trembling head, and her hands groped feebly in the air.

She longed to get away from the place, but her feet moved slowly. She looked around to find something to use as a staff.

After a few moments, with tremendous will power, she managed to overcome her faintness.

IV

A week later, old Faustina wandered up the steep hills on the island of Capri. It was a warm day, and she was feeling old and feeble as she laboured up the winding roads and hewn-out steps in the mountain which led to Tiberius's villa.

This feeling increased when she noticed how much everything had changed during the time she'd been away. In the past, crowds of people had gathered on these steps: they used to swarm with senators, who were carried by giant Libyans; with messengers from the provinces attended by long processions of slaves; with people looking for work; with noblemen invited to the emperor's feasts.

But today the steps and passages were entirely deserted. Grey-greenish lizards were the only living things the old woman saw in her path.

She was amazed to see that everything already appeared to be going to ruin. The emperor can't have been ill for more than two months, yet the grass had already taken root in the cracks between the marble stones. Rare flowers planted in beautiful vases were already withered, and mischievous weeds, which no one had taken the trouble to pull out, had broken through the wall here and there.

But to her the most singular thing of all was the entire absence of people. Even if strangers were forbidden to come to the island, there should still be attendants: the endless crowds of soldiers and slaves; of dancers and musicians; of cooks and stewards; of palace-sentinels and gardeners who belonged to the emperor's household.

When Faustina reached the upper terrace, she caught sight of two slaves who sat on the steps in front of the villa. As she approached, they rose and bowed to her.

"Hello, dear Faustina!" said one of them. "A god has sent you to lighten our sorrows."

"What does this mean, Milo?" asked Faustina. "Why is it so deserted here? They told me that Tiberius still lives on Capri."

"The emperor has driven away all his slaves. He thinks one of us gave him poisoned wine to drink, which brought on the illness. He would have driven even Tito and I away if we hadn't refused to obey him. As you know, we've served the emperor and his mother all our lives."

"Where are the senators and field marshals?" asked Faustina. "Where are the emperor's close friends and all the fawning fortune-hunters?"

"Tiberius doesn't wish to be seen by strangers," said the slave. "Senator Lucius and Marco, Commander of the Life Guard, come here every day and receive orders. No one else may approach him."

Faustina had gone up the steps to enter the villa. The slave went before her, and on the way she asked, "What do the doctors say about Tiberius's illness?"

"None of them understands how to treat it. They don't even know if it kills quickly or slowly. But I can tell you this, Faustina: Tiberius will die if he continues to refuse all food for fear of poisoning. And I know that a sick man can't stay awake night and day, as the emperor does, for fear he may be murdered in his sleep. If he'll trust you as he used to, perhaps you can encourage him to eat and sleep, and at least prolong his life for a few days."

The slave conducted Faustina through several passages and courts to a terrace where Tiberius used to sit and enjoy the views of beautiful bays and proud Vesuvius.

When Faustina stepped out onto the terrace, she saw a hideous creature with a swollen face and animalistic features. His hands and feet were swathed in white bandages through which half-rotted fingers and toes protruded, and his clothes were dirty and dusty. He clearly couldn't stand upright, but had been forced to crawl out onto the terrace. He lay by the far wall with his eyes closed, and didn't move when the slave and Faustina drew near.

Faustina whispered to the slave who walked in front of her, "But, Milo, what's this creature doing on the emperor's private terrace? Hurry and take it away!"

But she'd scarcely said this when she saw the slave bow to the ground before the miserable creature who lay there.

"Caesar Tiberius," he said, "at last I have some good news."

The slave turned towards Faustina, then shrank back, horrified.

He no longer saw a proud old woman, who looked so strong she might live to the age of a sibyl. She had suddenly withered into impotent age, and the slave saw a bent old woman with misty eyes and fumbling hands standing before him.

Faustina had heard that the emperor was terribly changed, but she'd never stopped thinking of him as the strong man she used to know. She had also heard someone say that this illness progressed slowly and took years to take effect. But here it had

advanced with such virulence that, in just two months, he was unrecognisable.

She tottered up to the emperor. She couldn't speak, but stood silently beside him and wept.

"Are you come now, Faustina?" he said without opening his eyes. "I imagine that you're standing here weeping over me. I dare not look up for fear that it's only an illusion."

Then the old woman sat down beside him. She raised his head and placed it on her knee.

Tiberius lay still, without looking at her. A sense of sweet peace enfolded him, and the next moment he sank into a deep sleep.

V

A few weeks later, one of the emperor's slaves came to the lonely hut in the Sabine Mountains. Evening was drawing in, and the vine-tender and his wife stood in the doorway watching the sun set in the distant west. The slave turned off the path, and came up to greet them. He took a heavy purse from his girdle, and laid it in the husband's hand.

"Faustina, the old woman you've been kind to, sends you this," said the slave. "She begs that with this money you'll buy a vineyard of your own, and build a house that doesn't lie as high in the air as the eagles' nests."

"Old Faustina still lives, then?" said the husband. "We've searched for her by gorges and cliffs. When she didn't come back to us, I thought she'd died in these wretched mountains."

"Remember," the wife interrupted, "I didn't believe she was dead. Didn't I say that she'd gone back to the emperor?"

This the husband admitted. "And I'm glad," he added, "that you were right. Not only because Faustina has become rich enough to help us out of our poverty, but also on the poor emperor's account."

The slave wanted to leave at once, to be back in town before dark, but the couple wouldn't allow it. "You must stay with us until morning," they said. "We can't let you go before you've told us what happened to Faustina. Why has she returned to the emperor? What was their meeting like? Are they glad to be together again?"

The slave agreed to stay. He followed them into the hut, and during the evening meal he told them all about the emperor's illness and Faustina's return.

When the slave had finished his story, he saw that both the man and the woman sat stock still – dumb with amazement. They both stared at the ground to hide the emotion in their eyes.

Finally the man looked up and said to his wife, "Don't you believe God has decreed this?"

"Yes," said the wife, "surely this is why our Lord sent us across the sea to this lonely hut. Surely this is why he sent the old woman to our door."

The vine-tender turned again to the slave. "Friend," he said, "please carry a message from me to Faustina. Tell her this, word for word. Your friend, the vine-tender from the Sabine Mountains, greets you. You know my wife the young woman. Didn't she seem fair to you and blooming with health? But she once suffered from the same disease that Tiberius now has."

The slave made a gesture of surprise, but the vine-tender continued with greater emphasis.

"If Faustina refuses to believe my word, tell her that my wife and I came from Palestine in Asia, a land where this disease is common. There, by law, lepers are driven from the cities and towns, and must live in tombs and mountain caves. Tell Faustina that my wife was born to diseased parents in a mountain cave. As a child she was healthy, but when she grew up she caught the disease."

The slave bowed, smiled pleasantly, and said, "How can you expect Faustina to believe this? She has seen your wife in her beauty and health. And she must know that there's no remedy for this illness."

The man replied, "It's in her best interest to believe me. But I have witnesses. She can ask the people of Nazareth, in Galilee. There everyone will confirm my statement."

"Perhaps your wife was cured through a miracle of some god?" asked the slave.

"Yes, that's right," answered the labourer. "One day a rumour reached the lepers who lived in the wilderness: 'Listen, a great prophet has come to Nazareth, in Galilee. He is filled with the power of God's spirit, and he can cure your illness just by laying his hand on your forehead!' But the sick wouldn't believe this rumour. 'No one can heal us,' they said. 'Since the days of the great prophets no one has been able to save a single one of us from this misfortune.'

"But there was one young lady among them who believed.

She left the others in search of the city of Nazareth, where the prophet lived. One day, as she wandered over wide plains, she met a tall man with a pale face and curly black hair. His dark eyes shone like stars and drew her towards him. But before he reached her, she called out to him, 'Don't come near me because I'm ill, but tell me where I can find the Prophet of Nazareth!'

"But the man continued to walk towards her, and when he stood directly in front of her, he said, 'Why are you looking for the Prophet of Nazareth?'

"'I want to ask if he will lay his hand on my forehead and cure my illness.' Then the man went up and laid his hand on her brow. But she said to him, 'How will it help me to have you laying your hand on my forehead? You surely are no prophet?'

"He smiled at her and said, 'Go now into the city at the foot of the mountain to see the priests.'

"The sick girl thought to herself, 'He's mocking me because I believe I can be healed. He can't help me find the prophet.' And she went on her way.

"Soon she saw a man who was going out to hunt, riding across the wide field. When he came near enough to hear her, she called to him, 'Don't come close to me; I'm ill! But tell me where I can find the Prophet of Nazareth!'

"'What do you want from the prophet?' asked the man, riding slowly towards her.

"'Only for him to lay his hand on my forehead and cure my illness.'

"The man rode nearer. 'What illness are you suffering from?' he said.

"'Surely you need no doctor to tell you! Can't you see that I'm a leper?' she said. 'I was born to diseased parents in a mountain cave.'

"But the man continued forward because she was beautiful and fair like a blossoming rose. 'You are the most beautiful maiden in Judea!' he exclaimed.

"'Don't you taunt me, too!' she said. 'I know my features are destroyed and my voice is like a wild beast's growl.'

"He looked deep into her eyes and said, 'Your voice is as clear as the spring brook's when it ripples over pebbles, and your face is as smooth as a soft satin sheet.'

"He rode so close to her that she could see her face reflected in the shining brasses that decorated his saddle. 'Look at yourself in here,' he said.

"When she did, she saw a face as smooth and soft as a newly-formed butterfly wing. 'What is this I see?' she said. 'This is not my face!'

"'Yes, it's your face,' said the rider.

"'But my voice, isn't it rough? Doesn't it sound like wagons being drawn over a stony road?'

"'No! It sounds like a zither player's sweetest songs,' said the rider.

"She turned and pointed towards the road. 'Do you know who that man is who's just disappearing behind the two oaks?' she asked.

"'He's the Prophet of Nazareth who you just asked after,' said the man.

"Then she clasped her hands in astonishment and tears filled her eyes. 'Oh, holy one! Oh, messenger of God's power!' she cried. 'You've healed me!'

"The rider lifted her onto his saddle, and they rode to the city at the foot of the mountain, where they told the priests and elders what had happened. They questioned the young woman carefully, but when they heard that she'd been born in the wilderness to diseased parents, the priests wouldn't believe she'd been healed. 'Go back to where you came from!' they said. 'If you've been ill, you'll be ill for the rest of your life. Don't come here to the city to infect the rest of us with your disease.'

"She told them, 'I know that I am well, because the Prophet of Nazareth laid his hand on my forehead.'

"When they heard this they exclaimed, 'Who is he that he should cure the sick? You've been deluded by evil spirits. Go back to your own kind, and don't bring death to us all!'

"They wouldn't declare her healed, and they forbade her to remain in the city. They decreed that anyone who gave her shelter would also be considered diseased.

"When the priests had pronounced this judgment, the young maiden turned to the man who had found her in the field. 'Where can I go now? Do I have to return to the lepers in the wilderness?'

"But the man lifted her up onto his horse, and said, 'No, you'll never go back to the lepers in their mountain caves. We'll travel together across the sea to another land, where there are no laws against the sick.' And they…"

But when the vine-tender had got this far in his story, the slave stood up and interrupted him. "You need not tell me any more," he said. "You know the mountains. Come with me, so I can begin my journey tonight. The emperor and Faustina can't hear your news a moment too soon."

By the time the vine-tender had guided the slave through the mountains and returned to the hut, his wife was still awake.

"I can't sleep," she said. "I'm thinking about how these two will get along: a man who loves all people, and a man who hates them all. It could be disastrous!"

VI

Old Faustina was in distant Palestine on her way to Jerusalem. She didn't want to entrust this mission of finding the prophet to anyone but herself. She thought, "We can't make this stranger help us with either force or bribes. But perhaps if someone falls at his feet and tells him how desperately the emperor needs him, he will help us. Only someone who genuinely suffers at Tiberius's misfortune can make an honest plea for him."

The hope of saving Tiberius had renewed the old woman's youth. She managed the long sea trip to Joppa without difficulty, and she didn't need to be carried to Jerusalem, but rode a horse. She appeared to stand the difficult ride as easily as the Roman noblemen, soldiers and slaves who travelled with her.

The journey from Joppa to Jerusalem filled the old woman's

heart with joy and bright hopes. It was springtime, and as they rode over the Sharon Plain on the first day's travel, it looked like a brilliant carpet of flowers. The second day's journey, when they came to the hills of Judea, was also filled with flowers. The winding road passed through hills of different shapes and sizes, which were planted with blossoming fruit trees. And when the travellers were tired of looking at the white and red flowers of the apricots and persimmons, they could watch young vine leaves pushing their way through dark brown branches. They grew so quickly, you could almost see it.

It was not only flowers and spring growth that made the journey pleasant; it was lovely to watch the crowds of people who were on their way to Jerusalem that morning. From all the roads and winding paths, from lonely hilltops and the most remote corners of the plain, travellers came. When they reached the road to Jerusalem, those who travelled alone formed themselves into groups and marched forward merrily. An elderly man rode on a jogging camel with his sons and daughters, sons-in-law and daughters-in-law, and all his grandchildren walking by his side. It was such a large family that it made up an entire village. Two sons brought an old grandmother, who was too weak to walk, and with pride she let herself be carried among the crowds, who respectfully stepped aside.

In truth, that morning would have brought happiness to even the saddest people. The sky wasn't clear, but overcast with a thin greyish-white mist, but no one complained at the lack of sunshine. The perfume of budding leaves and blossoms didn't penetrate the air as usual under this veiled sky, but lingered over roads and fields. And this beautiful day which, with its faint mist and calm breeze seemed almost like a tranquil night, conveyed its message to the hastening crowds; they travelled onwards happily yet seriously, singing old hymns softly and playing instruments that sounded like gnats buzzing or grasshoppers piping.

When old Faustina rode forward among all the people, she was infected by their joy and excitement. She drove her horse to go faster as she said to a young Roman who rode beside her, "I dreamed last night that I saw Tiberius, and he begged me not to delay my journey, but to ride to Jerusalem today. It appears that the gods were telling me to come this beautiful morning."

Just as she said this, she came to the top of a long mountain ridge where she had to stop. A large, deep valley-basin lay in front of her, surrounded by pretty hills, and from the dark, shadowy depths of the valley rose the massive mountain crowned by Jerusalem.

But today, the narrow mountain city with its walls and towers, which lay like a jewelled crown upon the cliff's smooth height, was a thousand times bigger. All the hills which surrounded the valley were topped with bright tents and swarming crowds of people.

It seemed that everyone was on their way to a great festival in Jerusalem. Those who had come a long way had already pitched their tents. Those who lived near the city were still travelling. They came streaming along the rocky heights like an unbroken sea of white robes, songs and holiday cheer.

The old woman watched the seething mass of people and the long rows of tent poles for some time, then she said to the young Roman who rode beside her, "Truly, Sulpicius, the whole nation must have come to Jerusalem."

"It looks like it," replied the Roman, who had been chosen by Tiberius to accompany Faustina because he had lived in Judea for many years. "They're celebrating the great Spring Festival, when people, both old and young, come to Jerusalem."

Faustina reflected a moment. "I'm glad we came here on a festive day," she said. "It must mean that the gods protect our journey. Do you think it's likely that the Prophet of Nazareth has also come to Jerusalem to join in the festivities?"

"You're surely right, Faustina," said the Roman. "He must be here in Jerusalem. This is indeed a decree of the gods. Although you're strong and fit, we'd be lucky to avoid making the long, hard journey up to Galilee."

He rode over to a couple of wayfarers, and asked if they thought the Prophet of Nazareth was in Jerusalem.

"We've seen him here every day at this time of year," answered one. "He must be here this year because he's a good and holy man."

A woman reached out and pointed towards a hill that lay east of the city. "Do you see the foot of that mountain covered with olive trees?" she said. "The Galileans usually pitch their tents there, and they'll be able to tell you more about the prophet."

They journeyed farther along a winding path to the bottom of the valley, then they began to ride up towards Zion's hill and the city. The woman who had spoken went with them.

The steep, climbing road was bordered by low walls, where countless beggars and cripples sat. "Look," said the woman, pointing to one of the beggars, "there's a Galilean! I remember seeing him among the prophet's disciples. He can tell you where to find him."

Faustina and Sulpicius rode up to the man, who was poor and old with a heavy, iron-grey beard. His face was bronzed by heat and sunshine. He wasn't begging; on the contrary, he was so engrossed in thought that he didn't even glance up at the passers-by. At first he didn't hear Sulpicius addressing him, so the Roman had to repeat his question several times.

"My friend, I've been told that you are a Galilean. Please tell me where I can find the Prophet of Nazareth!"

The old man gave a sudden start and looked around him, confused. But when he finally understood the question, he was seized with rage and terror. "What are you talking about?" he burst out. "Why do you ask me about that man? I don't know him. I'm not from Galilee."

The local woman now joined in the conversation. "But I've seen you with him," she protested. "There's no need to be afraid, but tell this noble Roman lady, who's the emperor's friend, where she can find him."

But the terrified disciple grew more and more upset. "Has everyone gone mad today?" he said. "Are they possessed by an evil spirit, since they keep asking me about that man? Why will no one believe that I don't know the prophet? I don't come from his country. I've never seen him."

He was beginning to attract attention, and a couple of beggars who sat on the wall beside him also began to argue.

"You were definitely among his disciples," said one. "We all know that you came with him from Galilee."

Then the man raised his arms towards heaven and cried, "I couldn't stay in Jerusalem today because of that man, and now they won't even leave me in peace out here among the beggars! Why don't you believe me when I say I've never seen him?"

Faustina turned away with a shrug. "Let's carry on!" she said. "The man is mad. We'll learn nothing from him."

They went farther up the mountain. Faustina was no more than two steps from the city gate, when the local lady told her to be careful. She pulled in her reins and saw a man lying in the road just in front of her horse's feet. It was a miracle that he'd not already been trampled to death by animals or people.

The man lay on his back and stared upwards with dull eyes. Even though camels trod beside his head, he didn't move. He was poorly dressed and covered with dust and dirt. In fact, he'd thrown so much gravel over himself that it seemed as if he was trying to hide and deliberately be trampled on.

"What does this mean? Why is this man lying here in the road?" asked Faustina.

Instantly the man began shouting to the passers-by, "In mercy, brothers and sisters, drive your horses and camels over me! Do not turn aside for me! Trample me to dust! I have betrayed innocent blood. Trample me to dust!"

Sulpicius caught Faustina's horse by the bridle and turned it to one side. "It's a sinner who wants to do penance," he said. "Don't stop for him. Leave these strange people to their own devices."

The man in the road continued to shout, "Set your heels on my heart! Let the camels crush my chest and the asses dig their hoofs into my eyes!"

But Faustina didn't want to ride past the miserable man without trying to help him. She stayed beside him.

The local woman pushed her way forward again. "This man was also one of the prophet's disciples," she said. "Shall I ask him about his master?"

Faustina nodded in agreement, and the woman bent down over the man. "What have you Galileans done with your master today?" she asked. "I meet you scattered on highways and byways, but I don't see him."

The man who lay in the dust rose to his knees. "What evil spirit has possessed you to ask me about him?" he said in a voice filled with despair. "You see, surely, that I've lain down in the road to be trampled to death. Isn't that enough for you? You still come to ask me what I've done with him!"

When she repeated the question, the man staggered to his feet and put both hands to his ears.

"Why can't you let me die in peace?" he cried. He forced his way through the crowds that thronged in front of the gate, and rushed away shrieking with terror, while his torn robe fluttered around him like dark wings.

"We seem to have come to a nation of madmen," said Faustina as she watched the man running away. These disciples of the prophet were making her feel depressed. Could a man who had such fools among his followers do anything for the emperor?

Even the local woman looked distressed, and she said very earnestly to Faustina, "Mistress, you must hurry with your search! I fear something terrible may have happened to the prophet, since his disciples are distraught and can't bear to hear him spoken of."

Faustina and her followers finally rode through the gate of Jerusalem on dark, narrow streets which were alive with people. It seemed well-nigh impossible to get through the city. People continued to stream tightly through the streets, forcing the riders to stand still. Slaves and soldiers tried in vain to clear the way.

"Truly," said the old woman, "the streets of Rome are peaceful gardens compared with these!"

"It's easier to walk than ride on these overcrowded streets," said Sulpicius. "If you're not too tired, I'd advise you to walk to the governor's palace. It's a good distance away, but if we ride we won't get there before midnight."

Faustina agreed at once. She dismounted, left her horse with one of the slaves, and the Roman travellers began to walk through the city.

This was much better. They pushed their way quickly towards the heart of the city, and Sulpicius showed Faustina a wide street nearby.

"Look, Faustina," he said, "if we take this street, we'll soon be there. It leads directly down to our quarters."

But as they were about to turn into the street, the worst obstacle stood in their way.

At the very moment Faustina reached the street that ran between the governor's palace, Righteousness' Gate and Golgotha, they brought a prisoner through it to be crucified. A crowd of wild youths ran in front of him to witness the execution. They raced up the street towards the hill, waving their arms and howling; they were about to observe something they didn't get to see every day.

Behind them came groups of men in silk robes, who appeared to belong to the city's elite. Then came women, many of whom were weeping. A gathering of poor and maimed people staggered forward with piercing cries.

"O God!" they cried. "Save him! Send your angel and save him! Send someone to help in his direst need!"

Finally, there came a few Roman soldiers on great horses. They kept guard so that none of the people could dash up to the prisoner and rescue him.

Directly behind them followed the executioners, leading the man who was going to be crucified. They had laid a heavy wooden cross over his shoulder, but he was too weak to support it. It weighed him down, forcing his body almost to the ground.

He held his head down so far that no one could see his face.

Faustina stood at the opening of the little alleyway and saw the doomed man's heavy tread. She noticed, with surprise, that he wore a purple robe and a crown of thorns upon his head.

"Who is this man?" she asked.

One of the crowd answered, "The man who wanted to make himself emperor."

"And he must die for something which is scarcely worth striving for?" said the old woman sadly.

The doomed man staggered under the cross. He dragged himself forward more and more slowly. The executioners had tied a rope around his waist, and they began to pull on it to hurry him along. But as they pulled the rope, the man fell with the cross on top of him.

There was a terrible uproar. The Roman soldiers did all they could to hold the crowds back. They drew their swords on a couple of women who tried to rush forward to help the fallen man. The executioners attempted to force him up with cuffs and lashes, but he was pinned down by the cross. Finally two of them took hold of the cross.

Then the man raised his head, and old Faustina could see his face. His cheeks were streaked by whiplashes and drops of blood tickled from his brow, which had been pricked by the thorn-crown. His hair hung in knotted tangles, clotted with sweat and blood. His jaw was set firm, but his lips trembled as if they struggled to suppress a cry. His eyes, tear-filled and almost blinded from torture and fatigue, stared straight ahead.

But behind this half-dead face, the old woman saw – as if in a vision – a pale and beautiful man with majestic eyes and gentle features. She was suddenly stricken with grief – touched by the man's misfortune and degradation.

"Oh, what have they done with you, you poor soul!" she burst out, and moved a step nearer while her eyes filled with tears. She thought her heart would burst from pity for the poor man. She, like the other women, wanted to rush forward and drag him away from the executioners.

The fallen man saw her come towards him, and he crept closer to her. It was as though he'd expected to find protection in her. He embraced her knees. He pressed himself against her, like a child who clings to his mother for safety.

The old woman bent over him, and as the tears streamed down her cheeks, she felt the most incredible happiness that he had come to her for protection. She put one arm around his neck, and wiped away his tears and blood with her fine linen handkerchief – as a mother would wipe away tears from her child's eyes.

But now the executioners were ready with the cross. They snatched up the prisoner. Impatient because of the delay, they dragged him roughly away. The condemned man groaned, but he made no resistance.

Faustina embraced him to hold him back, but her feeble old hands were powerless, and when she saw him being dragged away she felt as if someone had torn away her own child. "No, no! Don't take him from me! He must not die! He shall not die!" she cried.

She felt the most intense grief as he was led away. She wanted to rush after him. She wanted to fight with the executioners and tear him from them.

But with the first step she took, she was seized with weakness and dizziness. Sulpicius quickly put his arm around her to stop her from falling. On one side of the street he saw a little shop and carried her in. There were no benches or chairs inside, but the shopkeeper was a kind man. He helped her over to a rug, and made up a bed for her on the stone floor.

She was not unconscious, but she felt so dizzy that she couldn't sit up and had to lie down.

"She's made a long journey today, and the noise and crush in the city have been too much for her," Sulpicius told the merchant. "She's very old, and even the strongest people can't conquer age."

"This is a difficult day for everyone," said the merchant. "The air is almost too heavy to breathe. It wouldn't surprise me if a severe storm were on its way."

Sulpicius bent over the old woman. She had fallen asleep, breathing calmly. He walked over to the shop door, where he stood and watched the crowds while he waited for her to wake up.

VII

The Roman governor of Jerusalem had a young wife, and the night before Faustina entered the city this young wife had had a dream.

She dreamed that she was standing on the roof of her house looking down on the beautiful courtyard, which was paved with marble and decorated with rare plants, in an Eastern style.

But all the sick, blind and lame people from the whole world were gathered there. She saw people with the plague whose bodies were swollen with boils, lepers with disfigured faces, paralysed people lying helpless on the ground, and other wretched people writhing in torment and pain.

They all crowded up towards the entrance to get inside, and several of those at the front of the crowd pounded on the palace door.

At last a watchman opened the door and came out onto the threshold, and she heard him ask what they wanted.

They answered, "We seek the great prophet who God has sent to the world. Where is the Prophet of Nazareth, the master of all suffering? Where is the man who can deliver us from our torment?"

The watchman answered them in an arrogant and indifferent tone, as palace servants do when they turn away poor strangers. "Looking for this great prophet won't do you any good. Governor Pilate has killed him."

The young wife couldn't bear to hear the terrible cries of grief and moaning from the crowd in her dream. Her heart was wrung with compassion and tears streamed from her eyes. But as she began to weep, she woke up.

Again she fell asleep, and again she dreamed that she stood on the roof of her house looking down on the big square courtyard.

And this time the courtyard was filled with all the insane and soul-sick people in the whole world. Some were naked, some covered themselves with their long hair, and some had braided crowns of straw and robes of grass and believed they were kings; some crawled on the ground and thought they were beasts; some dragged heavy stones, which they believed were gold; and some thought that evil spirits spoke through their mouths.

She saw all these people crowd up towards the palace gate, and the ones who stood nearest to it knocked and pounded to get in.

At last the door opened, and the watchman stepped out on the threshold and asked, "What do you want?"

They cried out, "Where is the great Prophet of Nazareth, who was sent by God, who can restore our minds and souls?"

She heard the watchman answer them indifferently, "It's useless for you to seek the great prophet. Governor Pilate has killed him."

When they heard this, they shrieked wildly as beasts howl, and they whipped themselves in despair until blood ran onto the paving.

And when the young wife saw their distress in her dream, she wrung her hands and moaned. And as she moaned she woke up.

But again she fell asleep, and again in her dream she was on the roof of her house. Her slaves sat around her playing cymbals and zithers, white blossoms fell from the almond trees, and the delicate perfume of clambering roses filled the air.

As she sat there, she heard a voice. "Go over to the balcony and see who's waiting in your courtyard."

But in the dream she declined, and said, "I don't want to see any more of those who crowd my courtyard tonight."

Just then she heard the clanking of chains, the pounding of heavy hammers and the knocking of wood against wood. Her slaves stopped singing and playing, and hurried over to the railing to look down. The young wife followed them and looked down into the courtyard.

This time the courtyard was filled with all the poor prisoners in the world. Some had come from dark prison dungeons and were fettered with heavy chains; some worked in dark mines and came dragging their heavy planks; some rowed on war galleys and brought their heavy iron-bound oars. Those who were condemned to be crucified dragged their crosses; those who were to be beheaded carried broad axes; those who were forced to carry heavy loads like beasts had backs bleeding from lashes. The eyes of those who'd been sent away from home as slaves burned with homesickness.

All these unfortunate people shouted together, "Open, open!"

And the watchman who guarded the entrance stepped onto the threshold and asked, "What do you want?"

And, like the others, they answered, "We're looking for the great Prophet of Nazareth, who has come to the world to free prisoners and give slaves their lost happiness."

The watchman answered them in a tired, bored tone, "You can't find him here. Governor Pilate has killed him."

When he said this, the young wife heard such an outburst of scorn and blasphemy in her dream that she thought heaven and earth trembled. She was ice-cold with fright, and when she shivered she woke up.

She sat up in bed and thought to herself, "I can't bear another dream like this. I'll stay awake all night so I don't see any more of this horror."

But even while she was thinking this she started to feel drowsy, and she laid her head on the pillow and fell asleep.

Again she dreamed that she sat on the roof of her house, and now her little son was running around playing with a ball.

Then she heard a voice say, "Go over to the balcony and see who's waiting in your courtyard."

But the young wife thought, "I've seen enough misery tonight. I can't endure any more. I'll stay where I am."

At that moment her son threw his ball over the balcony and

clambered up on the railing. Then she was frightened. She rushed over and grabbed hold of the child.

But as she caught him she cast her eyes downward, and once more she saw that the courtyard was full of people.

This time she could see all the people on earth who'd been wounded in battle. They came with severed bodies, cut-off limbs and big open wounds, which oozed with blood, drenching the courtyard.

Beside them came all the people in the world who'd lost their loved ones on the battlefield: the fatherless who mourned their protectors; young women who cried for their lovers, and old people who sobbed for their sons.

Those at the head of the crowd pushed against the door, and the watchman came out, as before, and opened it.

He asked, "Why have you come to this house?"

And they replied, "We're looking for the great Prophet of Nazareth, who will end war and bring peace to earth."

The watchman said impatiently, "Stop pestering me! I've said it often enough. The great prophet is not here. Governor Pilate has killed him." And he closed the gate.

The young wife could now guess what awful cries of despair she was about to hear. "I do not wish to hear it," she said, and rushed away from the balcony. In that moment she woke up, and discovered that in her terror she'd jumped out of bed onto the cold stone floor.

Again she decided not to sleep any more that night, and again sleep overpowered her, and she closed her eyes and began to dream.

She sat once more on the roof of her house, and beside her stood her husband. She told him about her dreams and he laughed at her.

Again she heard a voice saying, "Go and see the people who are waiting in your courtyard."

And she thought, "I don't want to see them. I've seen enough misery tonight."

Just then she heard three loud raps on the gate, and her

husband walked over to the balcony to see who wanted to enter his house.

But no sooner had he leaned over the railing than he beckoned his wife over.

"Don't you know this man?" he said and pointed down.

When she looked down to the courtyard, she found that it was full of horses and riders; slaves were busy unloading asses and camels. It looked as though a distinguished traveller might have arrived.

At the entrance gate stood a large, elderly, gloomy-looking man.

The dreamer recognised the stranger instantly and whispered to her husband, "It is Caesar Tiberius. I'm sure of it."

"I recognise him too," said her husband. He placed his finger on his mouth, signalling that they should be quiet and listen.

They saw the watchman come out and ask the stranger, "Who are you looking for?"

And the traveller answered, "I seek the great Prophet of Nazareth, who has been given God's power to perform miracles. Emperor Tiberius calls him to free him from a terrible disease that no physician can cure."

When he'd spoken, the slave bowed very humbly and said, "My lord, don't be angry, but your wish can't be fulfilled."

Then the emperor turned towards his slaves, who waited below in the courtyard, and gave them a command.

The slaves rushed forward – some with handfuls of ornaments, others with pearl-studded goblets, others dragging sacks of gold coins.

The emperor turned to the slave who guarded the gate and said, "All this shall be his if he helps Tiberius. With this he can give riches to all the poor people in the world."

But the watchman bowed even lower and said, "Master, please don't be angry, but your request can't be fulfilled."

Then the emperor beckoned again to his slaves, and a pair of them hurried forward carrying a richly embroidered robe with a breastplate of jewels.

And the emperor said to the slave, "See! I offer him power over Judea. With this robe he can rule his people like the highest judge, if he will only come and heal Tiberius!"

The slave bowed even nearer to the ground, and said, "Master, it's not within my power to help you."

Then the emperor beckoned once again, and his slaves rushed up with a golden crown and a purple robe.

"See," he said, "with this the emperor promises to appoint the prophet his successor, and give him dominion over the world. He shall have the power to rule according to his God's will, if he will only stretch out his hand and heal Tiberius!"

Then the slave fell at the emperor's feet and said imploringly, "Master, it is not within my power to obey your command. The man you seek is no longer here. Governor Pilate has killed him."

VIII

When the young woman woke up, it was already daytime, and her female slaves stood and waited to help her dress.

She dressed in silence, then asked the slave who styled her hair if her husband was up. The slave told her that he'd been called out to judge a criminal.

"I'd like to talk to him," said the young wife.

"Mistress," said the slave, "it will be difficult during the trial. We'll let you know as soon as it's over."

She sat in silence until she was fully dressed and ready, then she asked, "Have any of you heard of the Prophet of Nazareth?"

"Yes, he's Jewish and he performs miracles," answered one of the slaves instantly.

"It's strange, Mistress, that you should ask after him today," said another slave. "He's the man who was brought here by the Jews to be tried by the governor."

She asked them to find out immediately what crime he'd been charged with, and one of the slaves hurried off. When she returned, she said, "They accuse him of wanting to be king, and they're asking the governor to crucify him."

When the governor's wife heard this, she was terrified and said, "I must speak with my husband or a terrible disaster will happen here today."

The slaves told her again that this was impossible, and she began to weep and shudder. One of them was so touched, she said, "If you write a message for the governor, I'll try and take it to him."

Immediately she took a stylus and wrote a few words on a wax tablet, which was given to Governor Pilate.

But she didn't get a chance to talk to him alone all day. When he'd dismissed the Jews, and the condemned man was taken to the place of execution, it was time for dinner. Governor Pilate had invited the commander of the Roman troops, a young orator and several others who were visiting Jerusalem for the festival.

The dinner wasn't very cheerful because the governor's wife sat silent and dejected the whole time, and took no part in the conversation. When the guests asked if she was ill or upset, the governor laughingly told them about the message she'd sent him that morning. He thought it was hilarious that she'd believed a Roman governor would let himself be guided by a woman's dreams.

She answered gently and sadly, "In truth, it was no dream, but a warning sent by the gods. You should at least have let the man live through today."

They saw that she was seriously distressed. She would not be comforted, no matter how hard the guests tried to distract her from her worries.

But after a while, one of them raised his head and said, "What's this? Have we sat at this table so long that the day is already gone?"

They all looked up and saw that a dim twilight had settled over the outside world. It was remarkable to see how the variegated play of colour which nature spread over the earth had faded slowly to a uniform grey.

Even their own faces lost their colour. "We look like the dead," said the young orator with a shudder. "Our cheeks are grey and our lips are black."

As this darkness grew more intense, the woman's fear increased. "Oh, my friend!" she burst out at last. "Can you see now that the gods were trying to warn you? They are angry because you condemned a holy and innocent man. Although he's already on the cross, he may not be dead yet. Let's take him down! I'll nurse his wounds with my own hands. Please let him be saved!"

But Pilate answered mockingly, "I'm sure you're right that this is a sign from the gods. But they don't let the sun lose its lustre because a Jewish heretic has been condemned to the cross. On the contrary, it will be for something important that concerns the whole kingdom. Who can tell how long old Tiberius…

He didn't finish his sentence because the darkness had become so profound he couldn't even see the wine goblet in front of him. He broke off and ordered the slaves to fetch some lamps immediately.

When it was light enough for him to see the faces of his guests, he couldn't help but notice how depressed they looked. "Look what you've done!" he said half-angrily to his wife. "You and your silly dreams have succeeded in driving away any happiness from the table. But if you really can't think about anything else today, tell us what you dreamed and we'll try to interpret its meaning."

The young wife didn't hold back, and while she related vision after vision, the guests grew more and more serious. They stopped drinking and sat with knitted brows. The only one who continued to laugh and to call the whole thing madness was the governor himself.

When the story was over, the young orator said, "Truly, this is more than a dream; today I saw, not the emperor, but his old friend Faustina march into the city. I'm surprised she hasn't already arrived here."

"I've heard a rumour that the emperor has been struck down

by a terrible illness," added the leader of the troops. "I think your wife's dream may well be a warning from the gods."

"There's nothing incredible about Tiberius sending messengers to summon the prophet to his sick bed," agreed the young orator.

The commander of the troops turned towards Pilate, now deeply serious. "If the emperor has summoned this miracle-worker, it would be better for you and for all of us if he found him alive."

Pilate answered irritably, "Has the darkness turned you into children? One would think you'd all been transformed into dream-interpreters and prophets!"

But the orator continued his argument. "It may not be impossible, perhaps, to save the man's life, if you sent a swift messenger."

"You want to make a laughing stock of me!" said the governor. "Tell me what would become of law and order in this land if they learned that the governor pardoned a criminal because his wife had a bad dream?"

"But it's the truth, and not a dream, that I've seen Faustina in Jerusalem," said the young orator.

"I'll take the responsibility of defending my actions before the emperor," said Pilate. "He'll understand that this 'prophet', who let himself be beaten by my soldiers without resistance, wouldn't have been able to help him."

As he was speaking, the house was rocked by a noise like powerful rolling thunder, and an earthquake shook the ground. The governor's palace stood intact, but a few minutes after the earthquake a terrific crash of crumbling houses and falling pillars was heard.

When the deafening noise stopped, the governor called to a slave, "Run to the place of execution and command in my name that the Prophet of Nazareth be taken down from the cross!"

The slave hurried away. The guests filed from the dining hall out into the open air, where they would be safer from further earthquakes.

No one dared to utter a word while they awaited the slave's return.

He soon returned and stopped in front of the governor.

"You found him alive?" asked the governor.

"Master, he was dead, and the earthquake happened the very moment he died."

The words were hardly spoken when two loud knocks sounded against the outer gate. The guests jumped and staggered back, as if there had been another earthquake.

A slave approached, and said, "It's the noble Faustina and the emperor's kinsman Sulpicius. They've come to beg you to help them find the Prophet of Nazareth."

A low murmur passed through the group and soft footfalls were heard. When the governor looked around, he noticed that his friends had stepped away from him.

IX

Old Faustina had returned to Capri to see the emperor. She told him her story, and while she spoke she hardly dared look at him. During her absence the illness had made the emperor even more disfigured, and she thought to herself, "If the gods had had any pity, they would have let me die before being forced to tell this poor, tortured man that all hope is gone."

To her astonishment, Tiberius listened to her with indifference. When she told him how the great prophet had been crucified the same day she'd arrived in Jerusalem, and how near she'd been to saving him, she began to weep under the weight of her failure. But Tiberius only remarked, "You are grieving over this? Ah, Faustina! After a whole lifetime in Rome, you still believe in sorcerers and miracle-workers, from your childhood in the Sabine Mountains!"

Then the old woman realised that Tiberius had never expected any help from the Prophet of Nazareth.

"Why did you let me make the journey to that distant land if you believed all the while that it was useless?"

"You are the only friend I have," said the emperor. "Why should I deny your prayer, so long as I still have the power to grant it."

But the old woman felt the emperor had taken her for a fool, and she wasn't impressed.

"Ah, this is your usual cunning!" she burst out. "This is just what I can't stand about you."

"You shouldn't have come back to me," said Tiberius. "You should have stayed in the mountains."

It looked for a moment as if these two, who had clashed so often, would be at war again, but the old woman's anger suddenly subsided. She could no longer quarrel seriously with the emperor. She lowered her voice again, but she couldn't completely give up on making her point heard.

"But this man really was a prophet," she said. "I saw him. When his eyes met mine, I thought he was a god. I was mad to let him die."

"I'm glad you let him die," said Tiberius. "He was a traitor and a dangerous anarchist."

Faustina was about to have another outburst – then she checked herself.

"I've spoken to many of his friends in Jerusalem," she said. "He didn't commit the crimes he was accused of."

"Even if he didn't commit these crimes, he was surely no better than anyone else," said the emperor wearily. "Are there any people who haven't deserved death a thousand times in their lifetime?"

These remarks convinced Faustina to do something she'd been hesitating about until now. "I'll show you proof of his power," she said. "I told you that I laid my handkerchief over his face. It's the same handkerchief I'm holding in my hand. Will you look at it a moment?"

She spread the handkerchief out for the emperor, and on it he saw the shadowy outline of a human face.

The old woman's voice shook with emotion as she continued, "This man saw that I loved him. I don't know how he left an imprint of his portrait on my handkerchief, but my eyes fill up with tears when I see it."

The emperor leaned forward and looked at the picture, which appeared to be made up of blood and tears and the dark shadows of grief. Gradually the whole face stood out before him, exactly as it had been imprinted on the handkerchief. He saw drops of blood on the forehead, the piercing crown of thorns, hair which was matted with blood, and the mouth with lips that seemed to quiver in agony.

He bent down closer and closer to the picture. The face stood out clearer and clearer. Suddenly, from the shadowy outlines, he saw the eyes sparkle with hidden life. And while they spoke to him of the most terrible suffering, they also revealed a purity and sublimity that he'd never seen before.

He lay on his couch and considered the picture. "Is this a mortal?" he said softly and slowly. "Is this a mortal?"

Again he lay still and regarded the picture. Tears began to stream down his cheeks. "Although I don't know you, I mourn your death," he whispered.

"Faustina!" he cried out at last. "Why did you let this man die? He would have healed me!" And again he was lost in the picture.

"If you can't help me regain my health," he said after a moment, "I can still avenge your murder. My hand shall rest heavily upon those who have robbed me of you!"

Again he lay still for a long time, then he slid down to the floor and knelt before the picture.

"You are a man!" he said. "You are what I never dreamed I would see." He pointed to his disfigured face and crumbling hands. "I and all others are wild beasts and monsters, but you are a man."

He bowed his head so low before the picture that it touched the floor. "Have pity on me, although I didn't know you," he sobbed, and his tears watered the stones. "If you had lived, your glance alone would have healed me," he said.

The poor old woman was terrified now. It would have been wiser not to show the emperor the picture, she thought. She'd been afraid all along that if he saw it he'd be overwhelmed with grief. In her despair over the emperor's sadness, she snatched the picture away from him.

Then the emperor looked up, and his features were transformed! He looked just as he did before the illness. It seemed as if the illness had been rooted and sustained by his hatred of humankind, and had been forced to flee the very moment he felt love and compassion.

The following day Tiberius despatched three messengers.

The first messenger travelled to Rome to command the Senate to investigate the Governor of Palestine, and punish him if he was oppressing his people and condemning the innocent to death.

The second messenger went to the vine-tender and his wife to thank them and reward them for the advice they had given the emperor, and to tell them how everything had turned out.

When they had heard the full story, they were very moved and the vine-tender said, "I'll wonder for the rest of my life what would have happened if the prophet and the emperor had met."

The woman replied, "It couldn't have happened any other way. God knew such a meeting would have been too much for this world."

The third messenger travelled to Palestine and brought some of Jesus' disciples back with him to Capri, where they began to share their master's teachings.

When the disciples reached Capri, old Faustina lay on her death bed, but they had time to baptise her as a follower of the great prophet. And she was baptised "Veronica", which means "true image", because she had been entrusted to share their saviour's portrait with humankind.

Robin Redbreast

Once upon a time God created the world. He not only made heaven and earth, but all the animals and plants, as well as giving them their names.

There have been many legends about that time, and if we knew them all we would know everything that we no longer understand about our world.

One day, as God sat in paradise painting little birds, the colours in his paint pot ran out. The goldfinch would have had no colour if God hadn't wiped all his paint brushes on its feathers.

The donkey was given long ears on the same day because he couldn't remember his name. No sooner had he taken a few steps over the meadows of paradise than he forgot, and he had to come back three times to ask his name. At last God got quite impatient, took him by the ears, and said, "Your name is ass, ass, ass!" And while he said this, God pulled both of the donkey's ears so he could hear better and remember what he was told.

It was on the same day that the bee was punished. Now, when the bee was created, she immediately began to gather honey, and the animals and human beings who smelled her delicious honey came along to taste it. But the bee wanted to keep it all for herself, so she used her poisonous sting to chase away every living creature that approached her hive. God saw this and at once summoned the bee to be punished. "I gave you the gift of gathering honey, which is the sweetest thing in all creation," he said, "but I did not give you the right to be cruel to your neighbour. Remember, from now on, that every time you sting a creature who wants to taste your honey, you will die."

It was at that time, too, that the cricket became blind and the ant lost her wings; so many strange things happened on that day!

God sat there, big and gentle, planning and creating all day long, and towards evening he decided to make a little grey bird. "Remember your name is Robin Redbreast," he said to the bird as soon as it was finished. Then he held it in the palm of his open hand and let it fly.

After the bird had been testing his wings for a while, and exploring the beautiful world where he was going to live, he became curious to see what he looked like. He noticed that he was entirely grey and that his breast was just as grey as the rest of him. Robin Redbreast twisted and turned in all directions as he viewed himself in the mirror of a clear lake, but he couldn't find a single red feather. Then he flew back to God.

God sat there on his throne, big and gentle. Out of his hands flew butterflies that fluttered around his head; doves cooed on his shoulders, and out of the earth beneath him grew roses, lilies and daisies.

The little bird's heart beat heavily with fright, but with easy curves he flew nearer and nearer to God, until at last he rested on God's hand. Then God asked what the little bird wanted.

"I only wish to ask you about one thing," said the little bird.

"What do you want to know?" said God.

"Why am I called Redbreast when I'm grey from my bill to the very end of my tail? Why am I called Redbreast when I don't possess one single red feather?" The bird looked beseechingly at God with his tiny black eyes then turned his head. He saw pheasants, all red under a sprinkle of gold dust; parrots with marvellous red neckbands; cockerels with red combs; to say nothing about the butterflies, goldfinches and red roses! And he thought how little red he needed – just one tiny drop of colour on his breast and he, too, would be a beautiful bird, and his name would suit him.

"Why should I be called Redbreast when I'm so entirely grey?" asked the bird once again, and waited for God to say, "Ah, my friend, I see that I forgot to paint your breast feathers red, but wait a moment and it shall be done."

But God only smiled a little and said, "I've called you Robin Redbreast, and Robin Redbreast shall be your name; you must earn your red breast feathers." Then he lifted his hand and let the bird fly once more out into the world.

The bird flew down from paradise, deep in thought.

What could a little bird like him do to earn red feathers? The only thing he could think of was to make his nest in a rose bush. He built it in deep among the thorns, as if he was waiting for a rose to grow by his throat and give him colour.

Countless years had come and gone since that day, which was the happiest in the world. People had already advanced so far that they'd learned to cultivate the earth and sail the seas. They'd made clothes and ornaments, and had long since learned to build big temples and great cities such as Thebes, Rome and Jerusalem.

Then a new day dawned, one that will long be remembered in the world's history. On the morning of this day, Robin Redbreast sat on a bare little hillock outside Jerusalem's walls and sang to his young ones, who rested in a tiny nest in a rose bush.

Robin Redbreast told the little ones all about that wonderful day of creation, and how God had named everything, just as each Redbreast had told the story since the first bird had heard God's word and flown from his hand. "And mark you," he ended sadly, "so many years have gone by, so many roses have bloomed, so many little birds have hatched since Creation Day, but Robin Redbreast is still a little grey bird. He has not yet succeeded in gaining his red feathers."

The little ones opened their tiny bills, and asked if their ancestors had never tried to do anything great to earn the priceless red colour.

"We've all done what we could," said the little bird, "but we've all failed. One day the first Robin Redbreast met another bird exactly like himself, and loved it so strongly that he could feel his breast burn. 'Ah!' he thought, 'now I understand! God meant that I should love with so much passion that my breast glows red from the warmth of love that lives in my heart.' But he was wrong, as were all the others who came after him, and as you will be too."

The little ones twittered, utterly bewildered, and already felt sad that they would have no red to liven up their downy grey breasts.

"We also hoped singing would help us," said the grown-up bird. "The first Robin Redbreast sang until his heart swelled within him, he was so carried away, and he dared to hope again.

'Ah!' he thought, 'the glow of the song that lives in my soul will colour my breast feathers red.' But he was wrong, as were all the others who came after him, and as you will be too."

Again he heard a sad "peep" from the young ones.

"We've also counted on our courage and valour," said the bird. "The first Robin Redbreast fought bravely with other birds, until his breast flamed with the pride of conquest. 'Ah!' he thought, 'my breast feathers will become red from the love of battle which burns in my heart.' But he was wrong, as were all the others who came after him, and as you will be too."

The young ones peeped courageously that they still wanted to try and win the much sought-after prize, but the bird answered them sorrowfully that it would be impossible. What could they do when so many splendid ancestors had missed the mark? What could they do more than love, sing and fight? What could... The little bird stopped short as a crowd of people marched out of the gates of Jerusalem, and the procession rushed towards the hillock where the bird had its nest. There were riders on proud horses, soldiers with long spears, executioners with nails and hammers. There were judges and priests in the procession, weeping women, and, above all, a mob of mad people running around and howling.

The little grey bird sat trembling on the edge of his nest. He was terrified that the little rose bush would be trampled on and his young ones killed!

"Be careful!" he cried to the little defenceless chicks. "Stick together and stay quiet. Here comes a horse that will ride right over us! Here comes a warrior with iron-shod sandals! Here comes the whole wild, storming mob!"

Suddenly the bird stopped his cry of warning and grew calm and quiet. He almost forgot the danger hovering around him. He hopped down into the nest and spread his wings over the young ones.

"Oh, this is terrible," he said. "I don't want you to see this awful sight. Three criminals are going to be crucified!" And he spread his wings so the little ones couldn't see.

They only heard the sound of hammers, the cries of anguish and the wild shrieks of the mob.

Robin Redbreast watched the whole spectacle, and his eyes grew wide with terror. He couldn't tear them away from the three poor men.

"How terrible people are!" said the bird after a while. "It isn't enough that they nail these poor creatures to a cross, now they've placed a crown of piercing thorns on the head of one of them. The thorns have cut his brow and he's bleeding," he continued. "And this man is so beautiful, and has such a kind, mild manner; surely everyone should love him. I feel as if an arrow were shooting through my heart when I see him suffer!"

The little bird began to feel more and more pity for the thorn-crowned man. "Oh, if only I were my brother the eagle," he thought. "I would draw the nails from his hands, and drive away everyone who tortures him with my strong claws!" He saw how the blood trickled down from the poor man's brow, and he could no longer sit quietly in his nest.

"Even if I am little and weak, I can still do something for this poor tortured soul," thought the bird. He left his nest and flew out into the air, striking wide circles around the crucified man. He flew around him several times without approaching, because he was a shy little bird, who'd never dared go near a human being. But little by little he gained courage, flew close to him, and pecked a thorn from the poor man's brow. And as he did this, a drop of blood from the man's face fell on his breast; it spread quickly and coloured all his fine breast feathers.

Then the man opened his lips and whispered to the bird, "Through your compassion you've won everything your kind has been striving for since the world was created."

As soon as the bird returned to his nest his young ones cried out, "Your breast is red! Your breast feathers are redder than the roses!"

"It's only a drop of blood from the poor man's forehead," said the bird. "It will vanish as soon as I bathe in a pool or a well."

But no matter how much the little bird bathed, the red

colour didn't vanish. And when his young ones grew up, the blood-red colour shone on their breast feathers too, just as it shines on every Robin Redbreast's throat and breast until this very day.

Our Lord and Saint Peter

After wandering on earth for many hard and sorrowful years, our Lord and St Peter arrived in paradise.

You can imagine how happy this made St Peter! Sitting on Paradise Mountain, looking out over the world made quite a change from wandering from door to door like a beggar; strolling around the beautiful gardens of paradise was quite different from roaming the earth, not knowing if they'd be given shelter on a stormy night or be forced to tramp the cold, dark streets.

St Peter hadn't always been certain that it would all end well. He couldn't help feeling doubtful and troubled at times; it had been almost impossible for him to understand why they had to suffer so much if our Lord was lord of the whole world.

He couldn't be tormented by yearning any more, and you can imagine how glad he was about this.

Now he could actually laugh at all the misery he and our Lord had been forced to endure, and how little they'd had to live from.

Once, when things were going so badly that St Peter thought he couldn't stand it any longer, our Lord had taken him to a high mountain and started to climb without telling Peter why they were there.

They had wandered past cities at the foot of the mountain and castles higher up. They had gone past farms and cabins, and had left the last wood-chopper's cave behind them.

At last they had reached the bare part of the mountain without greenery and trees, where a hermit had built a hut to shelter needy travellers.

Afterwards, they had walked over snow-fields where mountain rats slept, and come to sharp, piled-up blocks of ice, where scarcely a chamois antelope could pass.

Up there our Lord had found a little red-breasted bird that lay frozen to death on the ice. He'd picked up the bullfinch and tucked it under his robe, and St Peter remembered wondering if this was going to be their dinner.

They had wandered a long while on the slippery ice-blocks, and it had seemed to St Peter that he'd never been so near perdition; a deadly cold wind and a deadly dark mist enveloped them, and as far as he could see, there were no other living things around. And, still, they were only halfway up the mountain.

Then he begged our Lord to let him turn back.

"Not yet," said our Lord, "because I want to show you something which will give you courage to face all your sorrows."

And so they had gone on through mist and cold until they reached an interminably high wall, which stopped them from going further.

"This wall extends all around the mountains," said our Lord, "and you can't step over it at any point. No living creature can see beyond it because this is where paradise begins, and all the way up to the mountain's summit live the blessed dead."

But St Peter couldn't help looking doubtful.

"Inside there's no darkness or cold," said our Lord, "because it's always summer, with the bright light of suns and stars."

But St Peter found this hard to believe.

Then our Lord took the little bird that he'd found on the ice and, bending backwards, threw it over the wall so that it fell down into paradise.

And, to his surprise, St Peter immediately heard a loud, bright trill, and recognised the bullfinch's song.

He turned towards our Lord and said, "Let's return to earth and suffer everything we have to. Now I see that you're telling the truth: that there is a place where life overcomes death."

And they climbed down the mountain and began their wanderings again.

And it was years before St Peter saw any more than this one glimpse of paradise, but he always longed for the land beyond the wall. And now at last he was there, and he didn't have to strive and yearn any more. Now he could drink in bliss all day long from never-dying streams.

But St Peter hadn't been in paradise a fortnight before an angel visited our Lord on his throne, bowed seven times before him, and told him that St Peter wasn't well. He wouldn't eat or drink and his eyelids were red, as though he hadn't slept for several nights.

As soon as our Lord heard this, he went to look for St Peter.

He found him far away on the outskirts of paradise, lying on the ground as if he were too exhausted to stand. He had ripped all his clothes and rubbed ashes into his hair.

When our Lord saw him so distressed, he sat down on the ground beside him and talked to him, just as he would have done if they'd still been wandering around on earth.

"Why are you so sad, St Peter?" said our Lord.

But St Peter was overcome with grief and he couldn't answer.

"What is it that makes you so sad?" asked our Lord once again.

When our Lord repeated the question, St Peter took the gold crown from his head and threw it at our Lord's feet, as if to say that he wanted no further share in his honour and glory.

Our Lord understood, of course, that St Peter was too upset to know what he was doing, so he wasn't angry.

"You must tell me what troubles you," said our Lord just as gently as before, and with even more love in his voice.

But now St Peter jumped up, and our Lord realised that he was not only upset, but downright angry. He came towards our Lord with clenched fists and fury in his eyes.

"I want to be dismissed from your service!" said St Peter. "I can't remain another day in paradise."

Our Lord tried to calm him, just as he'd done many times before when St Peter had flared up.

"Of course you may go," he said, "but first tell me why you're so unhappy."

"I can tell you that I expected a better reward than this after we endured all sorts of misery down on earth," said St Peter.

Our Lord saw that St Peter's soul was filled with bitterness, and he felt no anger towards him.

"You are free to go wherever you will," he said, "if you'll only let me know what's troubling you."

Then, at last, St Peter told our Lord why he was so unhappy. "I had an old mother," he said, "and she died a few days ago."

"Now I understand," said our Lord. "You're upset because your mother hasn't come into paradise."

"That's right," said St Peter, and he was so overwhelmed with grief that he began to sob and moan. "I think I at least deserved that she be allowed to come here," he said.

Now that our Lord knew why St Peter was so upset, he also became distressed. St Peter's mother had not been entitled to enter the heavenly kingdom. She had hoarded money her whole life, and she never gave even a penny or a crust of bread to poor folk who knocked at her door. But our Lord knew that St Peter wouldn't be able to understand why his mother hadn't been allowed to enter paradise.

"St Peter," he said, "how can you be so sure that your mother would feel at home here with us?"

"You're only saying that so you don't have to listen to my prayers," said St Peter. "Who wouldn't be happy in paradise?"

"Anyone who doesn't feel joy in the happiness of others can't rest peacefully here," said our Lord.

"Then there are people other than my mother who don't belong here," said St Peter, and our Lord realised that Peter was thinking of him. And he felt terrible because Peter was so distressed he no longer knew what he was saying. He waited for a moment, expecting St Peter to apologise and realise why his mother wasn't fit for paradise. But the saint wouldn't give in.

Then our Lord called an angel and commanded him to fly down into hell and bring St Peter's mother to paradise.

"Let me see how he carries her," said St Peter.

Our Lord took St Peter by the hand and led him out to a

deep precipice, pitched steeply to one side. He only had to lean over the precipice a little to be able to look down into hell.

At first when St Peter glanced down, it was like looking into a deep well: as though an endless chasm opened under him. Then he could just make out the angel, who had already started his journey down below. St Peter saw how the angel dived fearlessly into the great darkness and spread his wings just a little to slow his descent.

But when St Peter's eyes had become a little more used to the darkness he began to see more and more. First he saw that paradise lay on a ring of mountains that encircled a wide chasm, and the souls of sinners lived at the bottom of this chasm. He saw how the angel sank down for a long time without reaching the bottom. He was terrified at such a long drop.

"Please let him come safely out of there with my mother!" he said.

Our Lord looked at St Peter with deep, sad eyes. "There's no weight too heavy for my angel to carry," he said.

It was so far down that no ray of sunlight could penetrate, and only darkness reigned. But it was as if the angel carried a little light with him so St Peter could his surroundings as he journeyed down.

It was an endless, black, stony desert. Sharp, pointed rocks covered the ground. There was not a green leaf, not a tree, not a sign of life.

But the sharp rocks were covered with condemned souls. They hung over the edges, where they had clambered when attempting to get out of the ravine; and when they had realised there was no escape, they'd remained up there, petrified with anguish.

Some of them sat or lay with their arms outstretched in endless longing, with eyes looking upwards. Others covered their faces with their hands, as if to shut out the hopeless horror around them. They were all completely still; not one of them had the power to move. Some lay in pools of water, perfectly still, without trying to pull themselves out.

But the most dreadful thing of all was that there were so many of them. It was as though the bottom of the ravine were made up of nothing but bodies and heads.

And St Peter was struck with a new fear. "He won't be able to find her," he said to our Lord.

Once more our Lord looked at him with the same sad expression. He knew, of course, that St Peter didn't need to worry about the angel.

But to St Peter it looked as if the angel was struggling to find his mother among all the lost souls. He spread his wings and flew back and forth, looking for her.

Suddenly one of the poor lost creatures caught a glimpse of the angel, and he sprang up and stretched his arms towards him and cried, "Take me with you! Take me with you!"

Then, all at once, the whole crowd was alive. All the millions upon millions who languished in hell roused themselves and raised their arms, begging the angel to take them with him to paradise.

Their shrieks were heard all the way up to our Lord and St Peter, whose hearts throbbed in sorrow for them.

The angel swayed high above the condemned souls, but as he flew back and forth they all rushed after him, so it looked as though they'd been swept up by a whirlwind.

At last the angel caught sight of the one he was searching for. He folded his wings over his back and shot down like a streak of lightning. The astonished St Peter gave a cry of joy when he saw the angel place an arm around his mother and lift her up.

"Bless you for bringing my mother to me!" he said.

Our Lord laid his hand gently on St Peter's shoulder, as if to warn him not to celebrate too soon.

But St Peter was ready to weep for joy because his mother had been saved. He didn't see how anything could part them now. And he was even happier to see that several of the lost souls had managed to cling on to her, so that they could also be carried to paradise. There must have been a dozen who clung to the old woman, and St Peter thought it was a great honour for his mother to help so many poor unfortunate beings out of perdition.

And the angel did nothing to stop them. He didn't seem at all troubled by his burden, but rose and rose, and moved his wings with no more effort than if he were carrying a little dead bird to heaven.

But then St Peter saw his mother trying to push away the lost souls that clung to her. She gripped their hands and loosened their hold, so that one after another tumbled down into hell.

St Peter could hear how they implored her, but the old woman didn't want anyone but herself to be saved. She freed herself from more and more of them, and let them fall down into misery. And as they fell, the whole abyss was filled with their wails and curses.

St Peter begged his mother to show some compassion, but she wouldn't listen and kept right on as before.

And St Peter saw how the angel flew slower and slower the lighter his burden became. St Peter was so frightened that his legs shook and he was forced to drop to his knees.

Finally, only one condemned soul still clung to St Peter's mother: a young woman who hung onto her neck and begged and cried in her ear to let her go along to paradise.

The angel had come so far that St Peter could stretch out his arms to receive his mother. He thought the angel only needed to make two or three more wing strokes to reach the mountain.

Then, all of a sudden, the angel held his wings perfectly still, and his expression became dark as night; because now the old woman had reached behind her to grip the arms of the young woman who was hanging round her neck. She clutched and tore until she managed to separate the young woman's clasped hands and free herself of this last soul.

When the young woman fell, the angel sank several fathoms lower, and it appeared as though he didn't have the strength to lift his wings again.

He looked down upon the old woman with a deep, sorrowful glance, his hold around her waist loosened and he let her fall, as if, now that she was alone, she were too heavy a burden for him.

Then he swung himself with a single stroke up into paradise.

St Peter lay for a long while in the same place and sobbed, and our Lord stood silently beside him.

"St Peter," said our Lord at last, "I never thought you would weep like this after you'd reached paradise."

Then God's old servant raised his head and answered, "What kind of a paradise is this, where I can hear the moans of my dearest ones and see the suffering of my fellow men below!"

A shadow of deep sadness fell upon our Lord's face. "All I wanted was to create a paradise for everyone, of nothing but light and happiness," he said. "Don't you understand? That's why I went down among men and taught them to love their neighbours as themselves. But if they can't do that, there can be no refuge for them from pain and sorrow in heaven or on earth."

The Sacred Flame

I

A great many years ago, when the city of Florence had only just been made a republic, a man named Raniero di Raniero lived there. He was the son of an armourer and had learned his father's trade, but he wasn't really interested in pursuing it.

This Raniero was the strongest of men. People said that he bore heavy iron armour as lightly as others wear a silk shirt. He was still a young man, but he'd already proven his strength many times. Once he was in a house with grain stored in the loft. Too much grain had been piled there, so one of the beams had broken and the whole roof was about to fall in. He raised his arms and held the roof up until people managed to fetch beams and poles to prop it.

People also said that Raniero never tired of fighting. As soon as he heard any noise in the street, he rushed out from his workshop, hoping to join in a fight. He fought as readily with humble peasants as with armoured horsemen in order to prove himself. He rushed into a fight like a lunatic, without counting his opponents.

Florence was not very powerful in his time. The people were mostly wool spinners and cloth weavers, and all they asked for in life was to be allowed to work in peace. There were a lot of strong men but they weren't quarrelsome, and they were proud of the fact that order prevailed in their city more than elsewhere. Raniero often grumbled because he hadn't been born in a country where the king gathered valiant men around him;

if he had been, he felt sure he would have attained great honour and fame.

Raniero was loud-mouthed and boastful; he was cruel to animals, harsh towards his wife and not good for anyone to live with. He would have been handsome if he didn't have several deep scars across his face. He was quick to jump to conclusions and quick to act, although often with violence.

Raniero was married to Francesca, who was the daughter of Jacopo degli Uberti, a wise and influential man. Jacopo had not been very keen to give his daughter to such a bully as Raniero and had opposed the marriage until the very last. But Francesca forced him to relent by declaring that she'd never marry anyone else.

When Jacopo finally gave his consent, he said to Raniero, "I've observed that men like you find it easier to win a woman's love than to keep it, therefore I demand this promise from you: if my daughter finds life with you so hard that she wants to come back to me, you will not prevent her."

Francesca said there was no need to demand such a promise, since she was so fond of Raniero that nothing could separate her from him. But Raniero gave his promise promptly. "Of one thing you can be assured, Jacopo," he said, "I will not try to hold on to any woman who wants to leave me."

Then Francesca went to live with Raniero, and they were happy for a while. When they'd been married a few weeks, Raniero decided to take up shooting. For several days he aimed at a painting that hung on a wall. He soon mastered the skill and hit the mark every time. So he thought he'd like to try shooting at a more difficult mark. He looked around for something suitable, but couldn't find anything except a quail that sat in a cage above the courtyard gate. The bird belonged to Francesca and she was very fond of it; but, despite this, Raniero sent a page to open the cage, and shot the quail as it flew into the air.

He was very pleased with himself, and he boasted about it to anyone who would listen to him.

When Francesca heard that Raniero had shot her bird, she

grew pale and stared at him. She was astonished that he'd wanted to do something that would make her so unhappy, but she forgave him promptly and loved him as before.

Then they were happy again for a while.

Raniero's father-in-law, Jacopo, was a flax weaver. He had a large and very busy workshop. Raniero thought that hemp was being mixed in with the flax in Jacopo's workshop, and he didn't think to stay quiet about it, but started to gossip about it around the city. When Jacopo heard this slander, he tried at once to put a stop to it. He let several other flax weavers examine his yarn and cloth, and they could all guarantee that it was the very finest flax. There was only a mixture in one pack, which had been prepared for sale outside Florence. Jacopo swore that this trickery had been carried out behind his back by one of his merchants, but he knew it would be hard to clear his name. He had always been famed for his honesty, and he was devastated that his reputation had been sullied.

Raniero, on the other hand, was proud that he'd exposed a fraud, and he bragged about it even in front of Francesca.

She felt terribly upset, and was as astonished as when he'd shot her bird. As she thought about it, she could suddenly see her love before her, like a large piece of shimmery gold cloth. She could see how big it was and how it shone, but a piece had been cut away from one corner so it wasn't as beautiful as it had once been.

Still, it was only damaged a little so she thought, "It will probably last as long as I live. It's so big it will never come to an end."

Again, for a while, she and Raniero were as happy as they'd ever been.

Francesca had a brother named Taddeo. He'd been in Venice on a business trip, and he'd bought new silk and velvet clothes while he was there. When he came home he paraded around in them. Now, in Florence it wasn't the custom to go about in expensive clothes, so lots of people made fun of him.

One night Taddeo and Raniero were out in the wine shops. Taddeo was dressed in a green cloak with a sable lining and a violet jacket. Raniero persuaded him to drink so much wine that he fell asleep, and then he took his cloak and hung it on a scarecrow in a cabbage patch.

When Francesca heard what Raniero had done, she was cross with him again. In that moment she saw the big piece of gold cloth – which was her love – and she saw it shrinking as Raniero cut away piece after piece.

After this, they patched things up for a while, but Francesca wasn't as happy as she had been; she was always worrying about what Raniero would do to hurt her next.

And, of course, this was not long in coming, because Raniero could never be at peace. He wanted people to talk about him all the time and praise his courage and daring.

At that time the cathedral in Florence was much smaller than the present one, and a big, heavy shield hung at the top of one of its towers. It had been put there by one of Francesca's ancestors. It was the heaviest shield any man in Florence had been able to lift, and all the Uberti family were proud that one of their own had climbed up the tower and hung it there.

So one day Raniero climbed up to the shield, hung it on his back, and brought it down.

When Francesca heard about this, she spoke to Raniero and begged him not to humiliate her family in this way. Raniero, who had expected her to praise his strength and daring, was very angry. He complained that she was never proud of his success and only ever thought about her own family.

"I do think of something else," said Francesca, "and that's my love. I don't know what will become of it if you keep on like this."

From then on, they often quarrelled, because Raniero nearly always did the very thing that Francesca found most distasteful.

There was a workman in Raniero's shop who was small and lame. He had loved Francesca before she was married, and still loved her. Raniero knew this, and liked to laugh about it in front of everyone. At last the man couldn't stand being ridiculed in front of Francesca any longer, so he rushed up to Raniero asking for a fight. But Raniero just smirked derisively and kicked him aside. After this, the poor man couldn't bear to live any longer, and hanged himself.

By this time, Francesca and Raniero had been married about a year. Francesca still saw her love before her as a shimmery piece of cloth, but it now had large pieces cut away from each side, so it was barely half the size it had been in the beginning.

When she realised this, she was very alarmed and thought, "If I stay with Raniero another year, he'll destroy my love. I'll become just as poor as I have been rich until now."

So she decided to leave Raniero's house and go to live with her father, in the hope that she'd avoid the day when she'd hate Raniero as much as she loved him now.

Jacopo degli Uberti was sitting at the loom with all his workmen busy around him when he saw her coming. He'd been expecting this to happen for some time, and he welcomed her. He instantly ordered everyone to stop working, and arm themselves and barricade the house.

Then Jacopo went to see Raniero. He met him in the workshop. "My daughter returned to me today and begged to live under my roof again," he said to his son-in-law. "And, after the promise you gave me, I expect that you don't ask her to return to you."

Raniero didn't seem to take this very seriously, but answered calmly, "Even if I hadn't given you my word, I wouldn't beg a woman who doesn't wish to be mine to come back to me."

He knew how much Francesca loved him, and said to himself, "She'll be back with me before evening."

But she didn't appear either that day or the next.

The third day Raniero went out and chased a couple of robbers who had long been bothering the Florentine merchants. He managed to catch them, and took them back to Florence as prisoners.

He remained quiet for a couple of days, until he was sure that his brave feat was known throughout the city. But it didn't turn out as he'd expected – it didn't bring Francesca back to him.

Raniero really wanted to take Francesca to court and force

her to return to him, but because of his promise it didn't seem right. He couldn't abide living in the same city as a wife who'd abandoned him, so he moved away from Florence.

First he became a soldier, and very soon he made himself commander of a volunteer company. He was always fighting, and served many masters. He soon became a renowned warrior, as he'd always said he would. He was made a knight by the emperor, and was considered to be a great man.

Before he left Florence, he had made a vow before a sacred image of the Madonna in the cathedral that he'd present her with the rarest riches he won in every battle. This image of Mary was always surrounded by valuable gifts from Raniero.

Raniero knew that all his deeds were known in his native city and by Francesca degli Uberti, and he was very surprised that she still hadn't come back to him despite his success.

At that time, troops were being summoned for the Crusades, to recover the Holy Tomb from the Saracens, so Raniero took the cross and left for the East. He not only hoped to win castles and land to rule over, but also to become such a renowned hero that his wife would love him again, and return.

II

The night after the fall of Jerusalem, there were great celebrations in the crusaders' camp outside the city. Almost every tent was filled with noise and rowdiness as the men had drinking bouts.

Raniero di Raniero sat and drank with some comrades, and his tent was even more riotous than the others. The servants barely had time to fill the goblets before they were empty again.

Raniero had the best reason for celebrating, because that day he'd won greater glory than ever before. In the morning when the city was besieged, he'd been the first to scale the walls after Godfrey of Boulogne; and in the evening he'd been honoured for his bravery in front of the whole corps.

When the plunder and murder were over, and the crusaders marched into the Church of the Holy Tomb carrying candles and wearing penitents' cloaks, Godfrey announced that Raniero should be the first to light his candle from the sacred ones that burn before Christ's tomb. Raniero took this to mean that Godfrey considered him the bravest man in the whole corps, and he was very happy to be rewarded like this.

As the night wore on, Raniero and his guests were in the best of spirits. A fool and a couple of musicians, who had wandered all over the camp entertaining people with their pranks, came into Raniero's tent, and the fool asked permission to tell a funny story.

Raniero knew that this fool was very popular, so he agreed to listen.

"It happened once," said the fool, "that our Lord and St Peter spent a whole day sitting on the highest tower in the castle of paradise, looking down on the earth. They had so much to watch, they hardly found time to exchange a word. Our Lord kept perfectly still the whole time, but St Peter sometimes clapped his hands with glee or turned his head away in disgust. Sometimes he applauded and smiled, other times he wept and sympathised.

"Finally, as it drew towards the close of day and twilight sank down over paradise, our Lord turned to St Peter and said that surely he must be satisfied by now. 'What should I be satisfied with?' St Peter asked impetuously.

"'Why,' said our Lord slowly, 'I thought you'd be pleased with what you've seen today.'

"But St Peter didn't want to be pacified. 'It's true,' he said, 'that for many years I've complained about Jerusalem being governed by unbelievers, but after all that's happened today, I think it might just as well have remained that way.'"

Raniero understood now that the fool was talking about the fall of the city that day. Both he and the other knights began to listen with greater interest.

"When St Peter had said this," continued the fool, as he cast a furtive glance at the knights, "he leaned over the pinnacle of the tower and pointed towards earth. He showed our Lord a city which lay upon a giant, solitary rock that shot up from a mountain valley. 'Do you see those mounds of corpses?' he said. 'And do you see the naked and wretched prisoners who moan in the night chill? And do you see all the smoking ruins of battle?'

"Our Lord didn't answer him, but St Peter went on with his lamentations. He said that he'd certainly been troubled about the city, but he'd never wanted it to come to this.

"Then, at last, our Lord answered, objecting, 'Still, you can't deny that the Christian knights have risked their lives with the utmost bravery,' he said."

The fool was interrupted by cheers from the gathered knights, but he hurried on.

"Oh, don't interrupt me!" he said. "Now I can't remember where I left off... ah! To be sure, I was just going to say that St Peter wiped away a tear or two that had sprung from his eyes and blurred his vision. 'I'd never have thought they could be such beasts,' he said. 'They've murdered and plundered the whole day long. I can't comprehend why you went to all the trouble of letting yourself be crucified in order to gain followers like that.'"

The knights took up the fun good-naturedly. They began to laugh loud and merrily. "What, fool? Is St Peter angry with us?" one of them shrieked.

"Be silent now, and let's hear if our Lord spoke in our defence!" said another.

"No, our Lord was silent. He knew from experience that when St Peter got going, it wasn't worth arguing with him. St Peter ranted on, as was his way, saying that there was barely any point in mentioning that, finally, these Christian knights had remembered which city they were in and had gone to church barefoot wearing penitents' robes; this spirit of peace and worship had been so brief. He leaned once more over the tower and looked down towards Jerusalem. He pointed out the Christians' camp outside the city. 'Do you see how your knights celebrate their victories?' he asked.

"And our Lord saw that there was revelry everywhere in the camp. Knights and soldiers sat watching Syrian dancers. Full goblets did the rounds while they threw dice, gambling over the spoils of war, and…"

"They listened to fools who told vile stories," interrupted Raniero. "Wasn't that also a great sin?"

The fool laughed and shook his head at Raniero, as if to say, "Wait! I'll pay you back." Then he begged once again, "No, don't interrupt me! A poor fool so easily forgets what he wants to say. Ah, it was this: St Peter asked our Lord if he thought these people were a credit to him. To this, of course, our Lord had to reply that he didn't think they were.

"'They were robbers and murderers before they left home, and robbers and murderers they still are today,' said St Peter. 'Today was pointless; no good will come of it.'"

"Come, come, fool!" said Raniero threateningly. But the fool seemed to consider it an honour to see how far he could go before they threw him out, and he continued fearlessly.

"Our Lord only bowed his head, as if acknowledging that he'd been quite rightly rebuked. At the same time he leaned forward eagerly and peered down with closer scrutiny than before. St Peter also glanced down. 'What are you looking for?' he asked."

The fool delivered this speech with very realistic expressions, so all the knights saw our Lord and St Peter before their eyes, and they wondered what our Lord had seen

"Our Lord answered that it was nothing in particular," said the fool. "St Peter gazed in the direction of our Lord's glance, but he couldn't distinguish anything other than a big tent, outside which a couple of Saracen heads were speared on long lances, and where a lot of fine rugs, golden vessels and valuable weapons, captured in the Holy City, were piled up. In that tent they were carrying on just as all the others were in the camp. A company of knights sat and emptied their goblets. The only difference might be that there was even more drinking and rowdiness here than elsewhere. St Peter couldn't understand why our Lord was so pleased when he looked down there that his eyes sparkled with delight. He'd rarely seen so many hard and cruel faces gathered around a drinking table. And the host who sat at the head of the table was the most dreadful of all. He was a man of thirty-five, frightfully big and coarse; his face was covered with scars and scratches; he had calloused hands and a loud, bellowing voice."

Here the fool paused a moment, as if he feared to go on, but both Raniero and the others liked hearing talk about them, and just laughed at his audacity.

"You're a daring fellow," said Raniero, "so let's see what you're driving at!"

"Finally, our Lord said a few words," continued the fool, "which made St Peter understand why he was so pleased. He asked St Peter if he saw wrongly, or if one of the knights really had a burning candle beside him."

Raniero gave a start at these words. Now, at last, he was angry with the fool, and reached out his hand for a heavy wine pitcher to throw at his face. But then he checked himself, so he could hear whether the fool planned to praise or insult him.

"St Peter saw now," narrated the fool, "that although the tent was lit mostly by torches, one of the knights had a burning wax candle beside him. It was a long, thick candle, one of the kind made to burn for twenty-four hours. The knight, who had no candlestick to set it in, had gathered together some stones and piled them around it to make it stand."

At this, the company burst into shrieks of laughter. They all pointed at a candle which stood on the table beside Raniero and was exactly like the one the fool had described. Blood rushed to Raniero's face, because this was the candle he'd been allowed to light at the Holy Tomb just a few hours before. He hadn't been able to decide whether or not to let it die out.

"When St Peter saw that candle," said the fool, "he realised why our Lord was so happy, but at the same time he couldn't help feeling a little sorry for his master. 'Oh,' he said, 'you're looking at the knight who leaped on the wall this morning immediately after the gentleman of Boulogne, and who was permitted to light his candle first at the Holy Tomb this evening.'

"'Yes!' said our Lord. 'And, as you see, his candle is still burning.'"

The fool talked very fast now, casting an occasional sly glance at Raniero. "St Peter couldn't help pitying our Lord. 'Don't you understand why he keeps that candle burning?' he said. 'He doesn't think of your suffering and death whenever he looks at it; he only thinks of the glory he won, being considered the bravest man in the troop after Godfrey.'"

At this, all Raniero's guests laughed. Raniero was very angry, but he, too, forced himself to laugh. He knew they would have found it even funnier if he hadn't been able to take a little fun.

"But our Lord contradicted St Peter," said the fool. "'Don't you see how careful he is with the light?' he asked. 'He puts his hand around the flame as soon as anyone raises the tent flap, for fear the draught will blow it out. And he keeps chasing away the moths which fly around and threaten to extinguish it.'"

The laughter grew merrier and merrier, because the fool was telling the truth. Raniero found it more and more difficult to control himself. He couldn't bear anyone jesting about the sacred candle.

"Still, St Peter was dubious," continued the fool. "He asked our Lord if he knew that knight. 'He doesn't often go to Mass or pray,' said St Peter. But our Lord couldn't be swerved from his opinion.

"'St Peter, St Peter,' he said earnestly. 'Remember that from now on this knight will become even more pious than Godfrey. Where can piety and gentleness be learned if not from my tomb? Raniero di Raniero will help widows and poor prisoners – you'll see. He'll care for the sick and despairing as he now cares for the sacred candle flame.'"

At this, the men split their sides with laughter; knowing Raniero and his way of life, it seemed ludicrous. Raniero found both the jokes and laughter intolerable now. He sprang to his feet to teach the fool a lesson. As he did this, he bumped so hard against the table – which was only a door set up on loose boxes – that it wobbled, and the candle fell down. It was evident immediately how desperate Raniero was to keep the candle burning. He controlled his anger, carefully picking up the candle and rekindling the flame, before rushing upon the fool. But the fool had already darted out of the tent, and Raniero knew it would be useless to pursue him in the darkness. "I'll probably bump into him another time," he thought, and sat down.

The guests had continued to laugh mockingly the whole time, and one of them turned to Raniero. "There's one thing that's certain, Raniero: this time you can't send the most precious thing you won in battle to the Madonna in Florence."

Raniero asked why he couldn't follow his old tradition this time.

"Surely you can't send the sacred candle flame to Florence!" said the knight.

Again the other knights laughed, but Raniero was now determined to undertake even the wildest mission, just to put an end to their laughter. He came to a conclusion quickly, called to an old squire, and said, "Get ready, Giovanni, for a long journey. Tomorrow you shall travel to Florence with this sacred candle flame."

But the squire bluntly refused. "I don't want to," he said. "How could I possibly travel to Florence with a candle flame? It would go out before I'd even left the camp."

Raniero asked one after another of his men, and received the same reply from them all. They didn't take his command seriously.

The foreign knights who were his guests laughed even louder and more merrily as it became clear that none of Raniero's men would obey him.

Raniero grew more and more agitated. Finally, he lost his patience and shouted, "This candle flame shall nevertheless be carried to Florence; and since no one else will ride there with it, I will do so myself!"

"Consider before you promise anything of the kind!" said a knight. "You ride away from winning a principality."

"I swear to you that I will carry this sacred flame to Florence!" exclaimed Raniero. "I shall do what no one else wishes to."

The old squire defended himself. "Master, it's another matter for you. You can take servants with you, but I would have to go alone."

But Raniero was now out of his mind, and didn't consider what he was saying. "I, too, shall travel alone," he said.

With this declaration, Raniero had made his point. Everyone in the tent had stopped laughing. Terrified, they sat and stared at him.

"Why don't you laugh any more?" asked Raniero. "This mission is mere child's play for a brave man."

III

The next morning at dawn Raniero mounted his horse. He was in full armour, but he'd thrown a coarse pilgrim's cloak over it to stop the iron overheating under the sun's rays. He was armed with a sword and club, and he rode a good horse. He held the burning candle in his hand, and he'd tied a couple of bundles of long wax candles to the saddle, to keep the flame alight.

Raniero rode slowly through the long, tent-lined street, and so far everything was going well. It was still so early that the mists rising from the deep valleys around Jerusalem hadn't broken, so Raniero rode forward through a white night. The troops were all sleeping and Raniero passed the guards easily. None of them called out his name because they couldn't distinguish him through the mist; the roads were covered with foot-high dust, which muffled the horse's tramp.

Raniero was soon outside the camp and set out on the road which led to Joppa. It was smoother here but he rode very slowly now because of the candle, which burned feebly in the thick mist. Big insects kept dashing against the flame. Raniero had to guard it constantly, but he was in the best of spirits and still thought his mission could be accomplished by a child.

Then, the horse got sick of the slow pace and started to trot. The flame began to flicker in the wind, and it didn't help that Raniero tried to shield it with his hand and cloak. It was about to go out.

He was determined not to give up so soon. He stopped the horse, sat still a moment and pondered. Then he dismounted and tried sitting backwards, so that his body shielded the flame from the wind. He managed to keep it burning; but facing backwards would make the journey more difficult than he'd first thought.

When he'd passed the mountains which surround Jerusalem, the fog lifted. He rode forward now in complete solitude. There were no people, houses, trees or plants – only bare rocks…

…and robbers. They were idle folk, who followed the crusaders without permission, and lived by thieving and plundering. They had lain in wait behind a hill, and Raniero – riding backwards – hadn't seen them until they surrounded him, brandishing their swords.

There were about twelve men. They looked wretched and rode poor horses. Raniero quickly realised he could escape them. And after his proud boast the night before, he was determined not to abandon his mission easily.

He saw no other means of escape than to compromise with the robbers. He told them that they would never manage to overpower him, since he was armed and rode a good horse. And, as he was bound by a holy vow, he didn't want to fight them, but they could take whatever they wanted without a struggle, if only they promised not to put out his light.

The robbers had expected a hard struggle and were very happy with Raniero's proposal. They started to grab his belongings. They took his armour and horse, his weapons and money. The only things they let him keep were the coarse cloak and the

two bundles of wax candles. And they kept their promise not to put out the candle flame.

One of them mounted Raniero's horse. When he noticed what a fine animal it was, he felt a little sorry for the rider. He called out to him, "Come, come, we shouldn't be too cruel towards a Christian. You can have my old horse to ride."

It was a miserable old nag of a horse. It was as stiff and slow as if it were made of wood.

When the robbers had gone at last, and Raniero had mounted the wretched horse, he said to himself, "I must have been be-witched by this candle flame. For its sake, I'm now travelling along the roads like a crazy beggar!"

He knew it would be wiser to turn back, because his mission wasn't really practical. But he was so keen to accomplish it, he couldn't resist the desire to go on. And so on he went, surrounded by the same bare, yellow hills.

After a while he met a goatherd who tended four goats. When Raniero saw the animals grazing on the barren ground, he wondered if they were eating earth.

This goatherd had once owned a larger flock, which had been stolen from him by the crusaders. So when he noticed a solitary Christian come riding towards him, he tried to attack him. He rushed up to him and struck at the candle flame with his staff. Raniero was so obsessed with keeping the flame alight that he couldn't even defend himself against a goatherd. He only drew the candle closer to him to protect it. The goatherd struck at it several more times, then he paused, astonished, and stopped. He noticed that Raniero's cloak had caught fire, but Raniero did nothing to smother the blaze and could only focus on protecting the sacred flame. Seeing this, the goatherd felt ashamed. He followed Raniero for a long time, and when the road narrowed, with a deep chasm on each side, he joined Raniero and led his horse.

Raniero smiled and thought the goatherd must think he was a holy man who had undertaken a voluntary penance.

Towards evening, Raniero began to meet people. Rumours of the fall of Jerusalem had already spread to the coast, and a crowd of people had immediately prepared to go up there. There were pilgrims, who had been waiting for an opportunity to go to Jerusalem for years; there were newly-arrived troops; but they were mostly merchants, hastening with provisions.

When the crowds saw Raniero, who came riding backwards with a burning candle in his hand, they cried, "A madman, a madman!"

They were mostly Italians, and Raniero heard them shouting in his own language, "Pazzo, pazzo!"

Raniero, who had kept himself well in check all day, became intensely irritated by these continuous shouts. He suddenly leaped off his horse and began to punch people. When they saw how heavy the blows were, they took to their heels, and Raniero was soon alone again on the road.

When Raniero had regained his composure, he thought, "In truth they were right to call me a madman." He looked around for the light. He didn't know what he'd done with it. At last he saw that it had rolled down into a hollow. The flame had gone out, but he saw fire gleam from a dry grass-tuft close beside it, and he knew that luck was on his side because the flame had ignited the grass before it had been snuffed.

"This might have been the inglorious end to a whole lot of trouble," he thought as he lit the candle and stepped into the saddle. He was starting to realise that his journey was unlikely to succeed.

That evening Raniero reached Ramle, and rode up to a place where caravans usually stopped for the night. It was a large covered yard surrounded by little stalls where travellers could tie up their horses. There were no rooms, but folk could sleep beside the animals.

The place was overcrowded with people, but the host found room and food for Raniero and his horse.

When Raniero noticed how well he was being treated, he thought, "I almost believe the robbers did me a service by taking my armour and horse. It's certainly easier to travel with my light burden if they mistake me for a lunatic."

When he had led the horse into the stall, he sat down on a sheaf of straw and held the candle in his hands. He intended to stay awake all night. But he had hardly sat down when he fell asleep. He was completely exhausted, and stretched out in a deep sleep and didn't wake till morning.

When he woke up he couldn't find the candle. He searched for it in the straw, but couldn't find it anywhere.

"Someone has taken it and put it out," he said. He tried to persuade himself that he was glad it was all over and that he didn't have to carry on with his impossible task. But as he pondered, he felt a sense of emptiness and loss. Never before had he longed so much to achieve something he'd set his mind on.

He led the horse out and groomed and saddled it.

When he was ready to set out, the host came out with a burning candle. He said in Frankish, "When you fell asleep last night, I had to take your light from you, but here it is again."

Raniero betrayed no emotion, but said very calmly, "It was wise of you to put it out."

"I didn't extinguish it," said the man. "I noticed that it was burning when you arrived, so I thought it was important to keep it burning. You can tell it's been burning all night by how much it's withered."

Raniero beamed with happiness. He thanked the host heartily, and rode away in the best of spirits.

IV

When Raniero left the camp at Jerusalem, he had intended to travel from Joppa to Italy by sea, but after his money was stolen he decided to make the journey by land.

It was a long ride. From Joppa he headed north along the Syrian coast, then he rode west along the peninsula of Asia Minor, then north all the way to Constantinople. From there it was still an extremely long way to Florence. For the whole journey Raniero had lived on contributions from pious people; it was mostly pilgrims travelling en masse to Jerusalem who shared their bread with him.

Although he nearly always rode alone, his days were neither long nor monotonous. He was always busy guarding the candle flame, so he could never feel at ease. The merest puff of breeze or raindrop would have extinguished it.

As Raniero rode over lonely roads, thinking only about keeping the flame alive, it occurred to him that he'd seen something similar once before; he'd seen someone watching over something as sensitive as a candle flame.

This memory was so vague at first that he wondered if he'd dreamed it. But as he rode on alone through the countryside, it kept recurring to him.

"It's as if I'd not heard about anything else my whole life long," he said.

One evening he rode into a city. It was after sundown, and the housewives stood in their doorways looking out for their husbands. He noticed one who was tall and slender with earnest eyes, and she reminded him of Francesca degli Uberti.

Instantly he realised what he'd been pondering over. He remembered that, for her, love was like a sacred flame, which she'd always wanted to keep burning, and which she'd constantly feared Raniero would quench. He was astonished at this thought, but grew more and more certain that it was right. For the first time he began to understand why Francesca had left him and that he couldn't win her back through fighting.

Raniero's journey was long, partly because he couldn't go out in bad weather, but sat in travellers' lodges guarding the candle flame. These were very trying days.

One day, when he rode over Mount Lebanon, he saw that a storm was brewing. He was riding high up among the cliff tops a long way from any town or village. Finally he saw the tomb of a Saracen saint on top of a rock. It was a small, square stone structure with a vaulted roof, so he decided to seek shelter there.

He had barely entered when a snowstorm blew up, which raged for two days and nights. It was so cold that he almost froze to death.

Raniero knew that there were heaps of branches and twigs out on the mountain, and it wouldn't have been difficult for him to gather fuel for a fire. But he considered the candle flame which he carried to be highly sacred, and he didn't want to light anything from it except the candles before the Madonna's altar in Florence.

The storm got worse and he heard thunder and saw gleams of lightning. Then a bolt of lightening struck the mountain just in front of the tomb and set fire to a tree, so he could light his fire without having to borrow from the sacred flame.

As Raniero rode on through a desolate stretch of the Cilician Mountains, he used up all his candles. The candles he'd brought with him from Jerusalem had long since been consumed, but he'd found new candles in Christian communities along the way.

But now even these resources were finally exhausted, and he thought this would be the end of his journey.

When the candle was so nearly burned out that the flame scorched his hand, he jumped off his horse, gathered branches and dry leaves and lit these with the last of the flame. But up on the mountain there was very little fuel to burn, and the fire would soon die out.

While he sat grieving that the sacred flame would die, he heard singing down the road, and a procession of pilgrims came marching up the steep path, carrying lighted candles. They were on their way to a cave where a holy man had lived, and Raniero followed them. Among them was a very old woman who was struggling to walk, so Raniero carried her up the mountain.

When she thanked him afterwards, he asked if she would give him her candle. She did so, and several others also gave him the candles they carried. He put them out, hurried down the steep path, and lit one of them with the last spark from the fire of the sacred flame.

One day at noon it was very warm, and Raniero had lain down to sleep in a thicket. He slept soundly, and the candle stood beside him between a couple of stones. When he'd been asleep a while, it began to rain, and this continued for some time without him waking. When at last he was startled out of his sleep, the ground around him was wet, and he hardly dared glance towards the light for fear it might have gone out.

But the light burned calmly and steadily in the rain, and Raniero saw it was because two little birds flew and fluttered just above the flame. They caressed it with their bills and held their wings outspread, protecting it from any drops of water.

He took off his hood immediately and hung it over the candle. He suddenly wanted to stroke the little birds and he reached out his hand. Neither of them flew away, but let him catch them.

He was astonished that the birds weren't afraid of him. "They know I only desire to protect something sensitive, so they don't fear me," he thought.

Raniero rode through the region of Nicaea in Bithynia. Here he met some western gentlemen who were leading recruits to the Holy Land, and among them was a wandering knight and troubadour named Robert Taillefer.

Raniero, in his torn cloak, came riding along with the candle in his hand, and the warriors began as usual to shout, "A madman, a madman!"

But Robert silenced them and addressed the rider. "Have you journeyed far like this?" he asked.

"I've ridden like this all the way from Jerusalem," answered Raniero.

"Has your light been extinguished many times during the journey?"

"The flame still burns that lit the candle I carried away from Jerusalem," said Raniero.

Then Robert Taillefer said to him, "I also carry a light, which I hope will always burn. But perhaps you, who have brought your light all the way from Jerusalem, can tell me how to keep mine alight?"

Raniero answered, "Master, it's a difficult task, although it seems unimportant. This little flame demands all your attention so you can't think of anything else. It will not allow you to have a sweetheart – in case you desire one; it will not allow you to sit down and enjoy a party. You must only think of the flame, and have no other happiness. But my main reason for advising you not to make the same journey as I have is that you can't relax for a single moment. No matter how many dangers you've guarded the flame against, you can't rest, because in the very next moment it may fail you."

But Robert Taillefer raised his head proudly and answered, "What you have done for your sacred flame I may do for mine."

At last Raniero arrived in Italy. One day he was riding through lonely roads up in the mountains when a woman came running after him and begged him to give her a light from his candle. "The fire in my hut has gone out," she said. "My children are hungry. Please give me a light so I can heat my oven and bake bread for them!"

She reached for the burning candle, but Raniero held it back because he didn't want anything except the candles before the image of the Madonna to be lit by that flame.

Then the woman said to him, "Pilgrim, give me a light; the flame I am bound by duty to keep burning is the life of my children!" And because of these words he let her light the wick of her lamp from his flame.

Several hours later he rode into a town that lay far up on the cold mountain. A peasant was standing in the road, and saw the poor wretch who came riding along in his torn cloak. He instantly stripped off the short robe he wore and flung it to Raniero, but it fell directly over the candle and extinguished the flame.

Then Raniero remembered the woman who had borrowed a light from him. He turned back to her and lit his candle again with sacred fire.

When he was ready to ride on, he said to her, "You say that the sacred flame which you must guard is the life of your children. Can you tell me the name of this candle's flame, which I've carried such a long way?"

"Where was your candle lit?" asked the woman.

"It was lit at Christ's tomb," said Raniero.

"Then it must be called Gentleness and Love of Humanity," she said.

Raniero laughed at the answer. He thought himself an unusual apostle of these virtues.

Raniero rode on between beautiful blue hills until he saw he was near Florence. He thought that he'd soon have to part with his flame. He remembered his tent in Jerusalem that he'd left filled with trophies, and the brave soldiers in Palestine who would gladly welcome him back to the business of war, leading them to new conquests and honours.

Then he realised that this didn't appeal to him any more; his thoughts were drawn in another direction.

He noticed for the first time that he was no longer the same man who had left Jerusalem. His journey with the sacred flame had forced him to spend time with peaceful, wise and compassionate people, and to abhor those who were savage and warlike.

It made him happy to think of people who worked peacefully at home, and it occurred to him that he would willingly move back to his old workshop in Florence and do beautiful, artistic work.

"This flame has reinvented me," he thought. "I believe it has made a new man of me."

V

It was Eastertide when Raniero rode into Florence. He had barely made it through the city gate – riding backwards, with his hood drawn down over his face and the burning candle in his hand – when a beggar leaped up and shouted the customary, "Pazzo, pazzo!"

At this cry a street urchin darted out of a doorway, and a tramp, who for a long time had done nothing but lie and gaze at the clouds, jumped to his feet. Both began shouting the same thing: "Pazzo, pazzo!"

Now that three of them were shrieking, they made a good deal of noise and woke up all the street urchins, who came rushing out from nooks and crannies. As soon as they saw Raniero in his torn coat on the wretched horse, they shouted, "Pazzo, pazzo!"

But Raniero was used to this. He rode quietly up the street, seeming not to notice their racket.

But they were not content with merely shouting, and one of them jumped up and tried to blow out the light. Raniero raised the candle high, while trying to spur his horse on and escape the boys. But they kept up with him, and did everything they could to put out the light.

The harder he tried to protect the flame, the more excited they became. They leaped upon one another's backs, puffed their cheeks out and blew. They flung their caps at the candle. It was only because there were so many of them all crowded on top of one another that they didn't manage to quench the flame.

This was the largest procession on the street. People stood at the windows and laughed. No one felt any sympathy with a madman who wanted to defend his candle flame. It was time for church, and many worshippers were on their way to Mass; they, too, stopped and laughed.

But now Raniero stood upright in the saddle in his attempt to shield the candle. He looked wild. The hood had fallen back and they saw his face, which was wasted and pale like a martyr's. He lifted the candle as high as he could.

The entire street was now one great swarm of people. Even the older ones began to join in the uproar. Women waved their shawls and men swung their caps. Everyone tried to extinguish the light.

Raniero rode under the vine-covered balcony of a house, where a woman was standing. She leaned over the lattice-work, snatched the candle and ran inside with it. The woman was Francesca degli Uberti.

The whole city burst into shrieks of laughter and shouts, but Raniero swayed in his saddle and fell to the ground.

As soon as he lay there stricken and unconscious, the street emptied of people. No one wanted to take responsibility for the fallen man. His horse was the only creature that stopped beside him.

As soon as the crowds had left the street, Francesca degli Uberti came out from her house with the burning candle in her hand. She was still pretty; her features were gentle, and her eyes were deep and earnest.

She went up to Raniero and bent over him. He lay senseless, but the instant the candlelight fell upon his face, he moved and roused himself; the candle flame had complete power over him. When Francesca saw that he had regained his senses, she said, "Here's your candle. I snatched it from you, as I saw how anxious you were to keep it burning. I knew of no other way to help you."

Raniero had fallen badly and was hurt. But now nothing could hold him back. He began to raise himself slowly. He wanted to walk, but wavered, and was about to fall. Then he tried to mount his horse. Francesca helped him.

"Where do you want to go?" she asked when he sat in the saddle again.

"I want to go to the cathedral," he answered.

"Then I'll accompany you," she said, "because I'm going to Mass." And she led the horse for him.

Francesca had recognised Raniero the very moment she saw him, but he didn't know who she was because he hadn't taken the time to notice her. He kept his gaze fixed on the candle flame alone.

They were absolutely silent all the way. Raniero thought only of the flame and of guarding it well in these last moments. Francesca couldn't speak, because she didn't want her fears to be true: she could only assume that Raniero had come home insane. Although she was almost certain of this, she preferred not to speak with him than to have her fears confirmed.

After a while, Raniero heard someone weeping nearby. He looked around and saw that it was Francesca degli Uberti who walked beside him, and that she wept. But Raniero saw her only for an instant and said nothing to her. He wanted to think only of the sacred flame.

Raniero let her guide him to the sacristy, where he dismounted. He thanked Francesca for her help, but still didn't look at her – only at the light. He walked alone up to the priests in the sacristy.

Francesca went into the church. It was the day before Easter, and all the candles stood unlit upon the altars as a symbol of mourning. Francesca felt that every flame of hope which had ever burned within her had now been blown out.

A deeply solemn mood prevailed in the church. There were many priests at the altar. The canons sat together in the chancel with the bishop.

After a while Francesca noticed there was a commotion among the priests. Nearly everyone who wasn't needed to serve at Mass stood up and went out into the sacristy. Finally the bishop went too.

When Mass was over, a priest stepped up to the chancel railing and began to speak to the people. He told them that Raniero di Raniero had arrived in Florence with sacred fire from Jerusalem. He told them what the rider had endured and suffered along the way, and he sang his praises.

The people sat spellbound, listening. Francesca had never felt so blissfully happy before. "O God!" she sighed. "This is greater happiness than I can bear."

The priest talked for a long time, and finally said boldly, "It may perhaps seem trivial now that a candle flame has been brought to Florence. But I say to you, 'Pray to God that he will send Florence many bearers of eternal light, then Florence will become a great power and be famed among cities!'"

When the priest had finished speaking, the doors of the church were thrown open and a procession of canons, monks and priests marched up the centre aisle towards the altar. The bishop came last, and by his side walked Raniero, in the same cloak that he'd worn during the entire journey.

But when Raniero crossed the threshold of the cathedral, an old man walked towards him. It was Oddo, the father of the man who had once worked for Raniero and had hanged himself because of him.

This man approached the bishop and Raniero, bowed to them, then said in such a loud voice that everyone in the church could hear him, "It is a great thing for Florence that Raniero has brought sacred fire from Jerusalem. Such a thing has never before been heard of, so many people will say it's impossible. Therefore everyone should see the proof and witnesses Raniero has brought with him to assure us that this flame was really lit in Jerusalem."

When Raniero heard this he said, "God help me! How can I produce witnesses? I made the journey alone. Deserts and mountain wasteland must come and testify for me."

"Raniero is an honest knight," said the bishop, "and we believe him on his word."

"Raniero must know himself that people will doubt him," said Oddo. "Surely he can't have ridden entirely alone. His little pages can testify for him."

Then Francesca degli Uberti rushed up to Raniero. "Why do we need witnesses?" she said. "All the women in Florence would swear on oath that Raniero speaks the truth!"

Raniero smiled, and his face brightened for a moment. Then he turned his thoughts and his gaze back to the candle flame.

There was a great commotion in the church. Some said that Raniero shouldn't be allowed to light the candles on the altar until his claim had been substantiated, including many of his old enemies.

Then Jacopo degli Uberti rose and spoke on Raniero's behalf. "I believe everyone here knows that no great friendship has existed between my son-in-law and I," he said, "but now both my sons and I will answer for him. We believe he performed this task, and we know that anyone who carried out such a mission is a wise, sensitive and noble-minded man who we are glad to receive among us."

But Oddo and many others had no intention of letting him reach the goal he'd long been yearning for. They gathered together in a close group and refused to withdraw their demand.

Raniero could see that if this developed into a fight, they'd immediately try to get at the candle. As he kept his eyes steadily fixed upon his opponents, he raised the candle as high as he could.

He looked extremely exhausted and distraught. It was clear that, although he planned to hold out to the very last, he expected defeat. Oddo's words had been a crushing blow. As soon as doubt was raised, it would spread and grow. He thought Oddo had already extinguished the sacred flame for ever.

Then a little bird came fluttering through the wide, open doors into the church. It flew straight into Raniero's candle. He hadn't time to snatch it aside, and the bird dashed against it and put out the flame.

Raniero's arm dropped and tears sprang to his eyes. At first he felt relieved; it was better this way than if people had put out the flame.

The little bird continued its flight into the church, fluttering frantically hither and thither, as birds do when they come into a room.

Simultaneously a loud cry resounded around the church, "The bird is on fire! The sacred candle flame has set its wings on fire!"

The little bird chirped anxiously. For a few moments it fluttered about like a flickering flame under the high chancel arches. Then it sank suddenly and dropped dead upon the Madonna's altar.

But the moment the bird landed on the altar, Raniero was there. He'd forced his way through the church; no one had been able to stop him. From the sparks which destroyed the bird's wings, he lit the candles before the Madonna's altar.

Then the bishop raised his staff and proclaimed, "God willed it! God has testified for him!"

And all the people in the church, both his friends and opponents, stopped doubting him. They cried with one voice, transported by God's miracle, "God willed it! God has testified for him!"

Only a legend now remains of Raniero, which says he enjoyed good fortune for the rest of his days, and was wise, prudent and compassionate. But the people of Florence always remembered him as Pazzo degli Raniero because they'd once thought he was insane. And this became his honorary title. He founded a dynasty, which was named Pazzi and still is to this very day.

It became a custom in Florence, each year, the day before Easter, to celebrate a festival in memory of Raniero's homecoming with the sacred flame, called the "Scoppio del Carro", when they let an artificial bird fly with holy fire through the cathedral. And if the bearers of this sacred fire who have lived in Florence and made the city one of the most glorious on earth followed Raniero as their model, as the legend suggests, they too will have learned to sacrifice, to suffer and to endure. The example set by Raniero, who carried holy fire from Jerusalem in dark times, is immeasurable.

The Christmas Rose

Robber Mother, who lived in Robbers' Cave up in Göinge Forest, went down to the village one day to beg. Robber Father, who was an outlawed man, didn't dare to leave the forest. She took with her five children, each carrying a sack on his back as long as himself. When Robber Mother stepped inside the door of a cabin, no one dared refuse to give her whatever she demanded, as she was not above coming back the following night and setting fire to the house if she hadn't been well received. Robber Mother and her brood were worse than a pack of wolves, and many a man felt like running a spear through them; but they never did because they all knew that Robber Father stayed up in the forest, and he would have wreaked vengeance if anything had happened to the children or the old woman.

As Robber Mother went from house to house begging, she came to Övid Cloister. She rang the bell of the cloister gate and asked for food. The watchman let down a small wicket in the gate and handed her six round bread cakes – one for herself and one for each of the five children.

While the mother was standing quietly at the gate, her youngsters were running about. Now one of them came and pulled at her skirt to say he'd discovered something for her to come and see, and Robber Mother promptly followed him.

The entire cloister was surrounded by a high, strong wall, but the child had managed to find a little back gate which stood ajar. When Robber Mother got there, she pushed the gate open and walked inside without asking permission, as was her way.

Övid Cloister was managed at that time by Abbot Hans, who knew all about herbs. Just within the cloister wall he had planted a little herb garden, and it was into this that the old woman had forced her way.

At first glance Robber Mother was so astonished that she paused at the gate. It was midsummer, and Abbot Hans' garden was so full of flowers that all the blues, reds and yellows were dazzling to the eye. But soon an indulgent smile spread over her face, and she started to walk up a narrow path that lay between many flowerbeds.

In the garden a lay brother walked about, pulling up weeds. It was he who had left the door in the wall open, so he could throw weeds on the rubbish heap outside.

When he saw Robber Mother coming in with all five youngsters in tow, he ran towards her at once and ordered them away. But the beggar woman walked right on as before. The lay brother couldn't think what to do other than run into the cloister and call for help.

He returned with two stalwart monks, and Robber Mother saw that now he meant business! She let out a perfect volley of shrieks, and, throwing herself upon the monks, clawed and bit at them; so did all the youngsters. The men soon realised she could overpower them, and all they could do was to go back into the cloister for reinforcements.

As they ran through the passageway which led to the cloister, they met Abbot Hans, who hurried to find out what all this noise was about.

He scolded them for using force and forbade them to call for help. He sent both monks back to their work, and although he was a weak, old man, he took only the lay brother with him.

He went up to the woman and asked in a mild tone if the garden pleased her.

Robber Mother turned defiantly towards Abbot Hans, expecting him to grab her. But when she noticed his white hair and bent form, she answered calmly, "First, when I saw this, I thought I'd never seen a prettier garden; but now I see that it can't be compared with one I know of. If you could see the garden I'm thinking of you would uproot all the flowers planted here and throw them away like weeds."

The abbot's assistant was hardly less proud of the flowers than the abbot himself, and after hearing her remarks he laughed derisively.

Robber Mother grew crimson with rage to think they didn't believe her, and she cried out, "You monks, who are holy men, must know that on every Christmas Eve the great Göinge Forest is transformed into a beautiful garden to commemorate the hour of our Lord's birth. Those of us who live in the forest have seen this happen every year. And in that garden I've seen flowers so lovely that I dared not lift my hand to pick them."

Ever since his childhood, Abbot Hans had heard it said that on every Christmas Eve the forest was dressed in festive glory. He had often longed to see it, but he'd never had the good fortune. He eagerly asked Robber Mother if he could come up to Robbers' Cave on Christmas Eve. If she would send one of her children to show him the way, he could ride up there alone, and he would never betray them – on the contrary, he would reward them in any way he could.

Robber Mother said no at first, because she was thinking of Robber Father and the danger he might face if she allowed Abbot Hans to ride up to their cave. At the same time her desire to prove that the garden she knew was more beautiful than the monk's got the better of her, and she gave in.

"But you can only bring one other person with you," she said, "and you must not try to trap us, as sure as you are a holy man."

This Abbot Hans promised, and then Robber Mother went on her way.

One day Archbishop Absalon from Lund came to Övid and stayed the night. The lay brother heard Abbot Hans telling the archbishop about Robber Father and asking him for a letter of pardon for the man, allowing him to lead an honest life among respectable folk.

But the archbishop replied that he didn't want to let the robber loose among honest folk in the villages. It would be better for them all if he remained in the forest.

So Abbot Hans told the archbishop all about Göinge Forest, which every year on Christmas Eve blossomed as if it were summer around the Robbers' Cave. "If these bandits aren't too bad to witness God's glories, surely we can't be too wicked to experience the same blessing."

The archbishop knew how to answer Abbot Hans. "This much I will promise you, Abbot Hans," he said, smiling, "that any day you send me a blossom from the garden of Göinge Forest, I will give you letters of pardon for all the outlaws you choose to help."

The following Christmas Eve, Abbot Hans was on his way to the forest. One of Robber Mother's wild youngsters ran ahead of him, and close behind him followed the lay brother.

It turned out to be a long and hazardous ride. They climbed steep and slippery paths, crawled over swamps and marshes, and pushed through thickets and brambles. Just as daylight was waning, the robber boy guided them across a forest meadow, skirted by tall, naked trees and green fir trees. Behind the meadow loomed a mountain wall, and in this wall they saw a door of thick boards. Abbot Hans realised that they'd arrived, and he dismounted. The child opened the heavy door for him, and he looked into a poor mountain cave with bare stone walls. Robber Mother sat beside a log fire that burned in the middle of the floor. Alongside the walls were beds of pine and moss, and on one of these beds Robber Father lay asleep.

"Come in, you out there!" shouted Robber Mother without rising, "and fetch the horses in with you so they don't catch cold."

Abbot Hans walked boldly into the cave, and the lay brother followed. It was a bleak, poor place, and nothing was done to celebrate Christmas.

Robber Mother spoke in a tone as proud and bossy as any well-to-do peasant woman. "Sit down by the fire and warm yourself, Abbot Hans," she said, "and if you have food with you, eat, because you wouldn't want to taste the food we forest people eat. And if you're tired after the long journey, you can lie down on one of these beds to sleep. You needn't be afraid of oversleeping. I'm sitting here by the fire keeping watch. I'll wake you up in time to see what you've come up here to see."

Abbot Hans obeyed Robber Mother and took out his food sack, but he was so tired after the journey he could hardly eat, and as soon as he lay down on the bed he fell asleep.

The lay brother was also assigned a bed and he dropped into a doze.

When he woke up, he saw that Abbot Hans had left his bed and was sitting by the fire talking with Robber Mother. The outlawed robber also sat by the fire. He was a tall, raw-boned, lazy-looking man. His back was turned to Abbot Hans, to imply that he wasn't listening to the conversation.

Abbot Hans was telling Robber Mother all about the Christmas preparations he'd seen on the journey, reminding her of Christmas food and games that she must have known in her youth, when she'd lived at peace with other people. At first Robber Mother answered in short, gruff sentences, but she gradually became more subdued and listened more intently.

Suddenly Robber Father turned towards Abbot Hans and shook his clenched fist in his face. "You miserable monk! Did you come here to coax my wife and children away from me? Don't you know I'm an outlaw who can't leave the forest?"

Abbot Hans looked him fearlessly in the eyes. "I intend to get a letter of pardon for you from Archbishop Absalon," he said. He'd hardly finished speaking when the robber and his wife burst out laughing. They knew well enough the kind of mercy a forest robber could expect from Archbishop Absalon!

"Oh, if I get a letter of pardon from Absalon," said Robber Father, "then I'll promise you that I'll never again steal so much as a goose."

Suddenly Robber Mother rose. "You sit here and talk, Abbot Hans," she said, "but we're forgetting about the forest. Now I can hear, even in this cave, how the Christmas bells are ringing."

She'd barely uttered the words when they all sprang up and rushed out. But in the forest it was still dark night and bleak winter. The only thing they could hear was a distant clank borne on a light south wind.

When the bells had been ringing a few moments, a sudden light penetrated the forest; the next moment it was dark again, and then the light came back. It pushed its way forward between the stark trees like a shimmering mist. The darkness merged into a faint daybreak.

Then Abbot Hans saw that the snow had vanished from the ground as if someone had removed a carpet, and the earth began to take on a green covering. The moss-tufts thickened and raised themselves, and the spring blossoms shot up their swelling buds, which already had a touch of colour.

Again it grew hazy, but almost immediately there came a new wave of light. Then the leaves of the trees burst into bloom, crossbills hopped from branch to branch, and woodpeckers hammered on the tree trunks until splinters flew around them. A flock of starlings alighted in a fir top to rest.

When the next warm wind came along, blueberries ripened and baby squirrels began playing on the branches of the trees.

The next light wave that came rushing in brought with it the scent of newly ploughed acres. Pine and spruce trees were so thickly clothed with red cones that they shone like crimson robes, and forest flowers covered the ground till it was all red, blue and yellow.

Abbot Hans bent down to the earth and broke off a wild strawberry blossom and, as he straightened up, the berry ripened in his hand.

A mother fox came out of her lair with a big litter of black-legged cubs. She went up to Robber Mother and scratched at her skirt, and Robber Mother bent down to her and admired her cubs.

Robber Mother's children let out perfect shrieks of delight. They stuffed themselves with wild strawberries that hung on the bushes. One of them played with a litter of young hares; another ran a race with some young crows, which had hopped from their nest before they were really ready.

Robber Father was standing out in a marsh eating raspberries. When he glanced up, a big black bear stood beside him. Robber Father broke off a twig and struck the bear on the nose. "Keep to your own ground, you!" he said. "This is my turf." The huge bear turned around and lumbered away.

Then all the flowers from foreign lands began to blossom. The loveliest roses climbed up the mountain wall in a race with the blackberry vines, and flowers as large as human faces sprang from the forest meadow.

Abbot Hans wondered which flower he should pick for Archbishop Absalon, but each new flower that appeared was more beautiful than the others, and he wanted to choose the most beautiful of all.

Then Abbot Hans noticed that everything was still: the birds hushed their songs, the flowers stopped growing and the young foxes no longer played. From far in the distance came faint harp tones and celestial song, like a soft murmur.

He clasped his hands and dropped to his knees. His face glowed with happiness.

But beside Abbot Hans stood the lay brother who had accompanied him, and he was thinking dark thoughts. "This can't be a true miracle," he thought, "since it's been revealed to criminals. This can't come from God, but must have been sent here by Satan. The Devil's power is tempting us and showing us an illusion."

The angel crowd was so near now that Abbot Hans saw their bright forms through the forest branches. The lay brother saw them too, but behind all this wondrous beauty he saw only dreaded evil.

Birds had been circling around Abbot Hans' head the whole time, and they let him hold them. But all the animals were afraid of the lay brother; no bird perched on his shoulder, no snake played at his feet. Then there came a little forest dove. When she saw that the angels were nearing, she plucked up courage and flew down onto the lay brother's shoulder and laid her head against his cheek.

He thought he was being tricked and corrupted by sorcery, so he struck out at the forest dove and cried in such a loud voice that it rang throughout the forest, "Go back to hell, where you came from!"

By then the angels were so near that Abbot Hans could feel the feathery touch of their great wings, and he bowed down to earth in reverent greeting.

But when the lay brother's words sounded, they stopped singing and the holy guests turned in flight. At the same time the light and warmth vanished in terror. Darkness sank over the earth like a blanket; frost came, all the plants shrivelled up; the animals and birds hurried away; the leaves dropped from the trees, rustling like rain.

Abbot Hans felt his heart, which had just a moment before swelled with happiness, now contracting in agonising pain. "I can never outlive this," he thought: "that angels from heaven were so close to me and were driven away; that they wanted to sing Christmas carols for me and were forced to flee."

Then he remembered the flower he'd promised Archbishop Absalon, and he fumbled among the leaves and moss to try and find a blossom. But he could only feel how the ground under his fingers froze and the white snow came gliding over the ground. Then he was even more distressed. He couldn't stand up, but fell prostrate on the ground and lay there.

When the robbers and the lay brother had groped their way back to the cave, they realised they were missing Abbot Hans. They lit torches from the fire and went out to search for him. They found him dead upon the blanket of snow.

When Abbot Hans had been carried back down to Övid, the monks saw that his right hand was locked tight around something he must have grasped at the moment of death. When they finally opened his iron grip, they found a pair of white root bulbs that he'd torn from among the moss and leaves.

When the lay brother who had accompanied Abbot Hans saw the bulbs, he took them and planted them in Abbot Hans' herb garden.

He guarded them the whole year to see if any flower would spring from them. But in vain he waited through the spring, the summer and the autumn. Finally, when winter had set in and all the leaves and flowers were dead, he stopped tending them.

But when Christmas Eve came again and he couldn't help thinking about Abbot Hans, he wandered out into the garden to remember him. And look! As he came to the spot where he'd planted the bare root bulbs, he saw that flourishing green stalks had sprung from them, bearing beautiful flowers with silver leaves.

He called all the monks outside, and when they saw this plant blooming on Christmas Eve, when all the others lay still in the ground, they understood that Abbot Hans had really picked it from the Christmas garden in Göinge Forest. The lay brother asked the monks to take a few blossoms to Archbishop Absalon.

When Archbishop Absalon saw the flowers that had sprung from the earth in darkest winter, he turned as pale as if he'd met a ghost. He sat in silence a moment, then said, "Abbot Hans faithfully kept his word and I shall also keep mine."

He handed the letter of pardon to the lay brother, who departed at once for the Robbers' Cave. When he stepped in there on Christmas Day, the robber came towards him brandishing an axe. "I'd like to hack you monks into bits, as many as you are!" he said. "It must be your fault that Göinge Forest didn't bloom again this Christmas."

"The fault is mine alone," said the lay brother, "and I will gladly die for it, but first I must deliver a message from Abbot Hans." And he drew forth the archbishop's letter and told the man that he was free.

Robber Father stood there pale and speechless, but Robber Mother spoke for him. "Abbot Hans has indeed kept his word, and Robber Father will keep his."

When the robber and his wife left the cave, the lay brother

moved in and lived all alone in the forest to meditate and pray that his hard-heartedness might be forgiven.

But Göinge Forest never again celebrated the hour of our Lord's birth; and of all its former glory, only the plant which Abbot Hans picked still survives today. It has been named the Christmas Rose. And each year at Christmas time she sends her green stalks and white blossoms up through the earth, as if she's never forgotten that she once grew in the great Christmas garden at Göinge Forest.